Country Library

COUNTRY DOCTOR

This picture of a small country town from the point of view of its doctor over the past forty years brings back vividly the ways and characters of a fast-vanishing world, which had hardly changed for the previous two hundred years. It was a world of small, often quite isolated, communities, of difficult times for farmers, and of primitive conditions not only for farm workers but also for many of the towns-people. Traditions die hard, and the community as a whole changed only slowly: the previous doctor had been there for forty years, and his time had seen few alterations — motor cars and the telephone were for the rich only, and people from twenty miles away were still 'foreigners'. Dr Barber recalls his early years in practice with affection and many amusing anecdotes, as well as offering a fascinating survey of the changes in medicine and even in diseases during his career.

For this new edition, Dr Barber has written about the other side of a country doctor's life, his off-duty days. Hunting and shooting were very much part of a doctor's expected social round, and he vividly recalls many pleasurable days spent in the Essex countryside.

'I strongly recommend Dr Barber's book as a straight-forward and sometimes delightful sketch, drawn from nature.' Frank Swinnerton, *Books & Bookmen*.

D0048025

COUNTRY DOCTOR

Geoffrey Barber

THE BOYDELL PRESS

© Geoffrey Barber 1973, 1974

First published 1974
Reprinted 1975

First published in COUNTRY LIBRARY 1985
by The Boydell Press
an imprint of Boydell & Brewer Ltd
PO Box 9, Woodbridge, Suffolk IP12 3DF

ISBN 0 85115 234 1

Some of the material in this book first appeared
in article form in the magazine *Update*

British Library Cataloguing in Publication Data

Barber, Geoffrey
    Country doctor – Rev. ed. – (Country Library)
    1. Physicians (General practice) – England
    – Dunmow (Essex) – History – 20th century
    I. Title   II. Series
    362.1'72'0924   R729.5.G4

Printed in Great Britain by
St Edmundsbury Press, Bury St Edmunds, Suffolk

CONTENTS

PREFACE

Long before the Ancient Mariner, old people have insisted on boring the young with tales of their own youth. Yet when driving home from shooting with my sons and passing some house which reminded me of my early days as doctor here, I would tell the tale for what it is worth. Again, as young partners came into the practice, there was bound to be reminiscence about a patient or his family: so that it was a pleasant surprise to be attacked simultaneously both by my family and my partners to write something of this down before 'it was too late'. Perhaps it was their tactful way of suggesting that I should get it out of my system, and so avoid telling the same story over again and again.

My predecessor Dr Tench in started practice here in 1891, and died shortly after I came to take over from him in 1930. I retired from the practice in 1967: I had hoped to make it up to 80 years between us, but there came an evening when I was facing an unfortunate woman who had a multitude of irrelevant troubles, and who was obviously in need of that long session of anxiety gamesmanship, and found that I was asking myself

'What am I trying to do with this woman?'

And the answer came back loud and clear:

'Get rid of her as quickly as possible.'

I realised that this must be the end. If I no longer enjoyed the work as I had always done, and no longer welcomed the challenge of the awkward patient or the difficult case, then it was time I made way for a younger and fresher doctor.

So there has been time to write down some of the anecdotes: they belong to a way of life which was very different, but I was young and eager and confident; and the small country practice was what I had chosen as my world.

CHAPTER I

ARRIVAL

Dunmow in 1930 was typical of many small market towns in the eastern counties. It was an agricultural neighbourhood, following much the same social and economic pattern as it had done for the last two hundred years, apart from the changes which had come in the first world war when a certain number of the men had gone abroad and come back with a widened experience of the world outside. Motor traffic had brought in a number of strangers ('foreigners') and a limited bus service had widened the horizon for the farm workers and their families.

Farming was at a very low ebb; many of the tenant farmers were becoming bankrupt, and the small owners were selling up. A number of buildings were derelict, and weeds and nettles reduced the crops. Hedges were overgrown and ditches were blocked, and rabbits swarmed to such an extent that there was often a headland of several yards quite bare of corn where it had been eaten down.

The cottages of the farm workers were without electricity, water or drains; in Dunmow itself there was a small private gas company; there was an even smaller local gas company in Thaxted. On fine Sunday mornings the manager climbed to the top of the little gasometer and sat there reading his paper, so as to give the housewives extra pressure to cook their Sunday dinners.

Half of my house was on the 'company water', the other depending on two pumps. The houses in the main street had a sewer, but my house like several others had a cess-pit: and outside the town this was the rule for the larger houses, with earth closets for the cottages. In the villages water was fetched from the village pump, and rain water was collected from the roofs in large butts: local streams and ponds were used, and I remember the distress of an old lady in a cottage half way between Dunmow and High Roding whose supply was a small pond outside her house. One hot dusty day a traction engine came by, and being short of water, the driver put down his hose into her pond and sucked it dry. She told me she would now have to walk two miles each way to get her water unless some kind person did it for her.

There was a daily bus to Chelmsford, but Bishop's Stortford and Braintree were served by 'the Dunmow Flyer', a very efficient little branch railway line of the old London and North Eastern Railway. At Bishop's Stortford the Cambridge express would wait for the connection, so that I could travel to Liverpool Street from Dunmow in considerably greater comfort and faster than today. As it was a single line, there was a 'staff' without which a train might not move out of a station. Each section of line between the small stations had its own staff and there used to be a ceremonial changing of these staffs as the train steamed into the station with the porter dexterously catching the used staff and handing the new one while the train was moving. He could just as well have done it at leisure later on when the train had stopped, and I suspect that the custom was continued as a showpiece for the occasional tourists.

Carrier vans were still running both to Bishop's Stortford and through the Rodings. These were covered horse drawn carts which went to and fro on certain days and whose driver would execute commissions either way. For the first ten years a Mr Campen used to call at the doctor's surgery with a large basket to collect the medicines which had been prescribed on the rounds of the previous day: when his horse died he did the same round on a bicycle with baskets in front and behind, and even towards the end he trudged on foot, but he usually got a lift.

There were very few telephones. The telephone in Dr Tench's house was an elaborate wall fixture in the 'back hall', with a Leclanche wet cell above it. The handle had to be squeezed to keep the circuit closed, and there was an extra earphone for the other ear as the caller's voice could be very faint when the battery went low. The other doctor's number was Dunmow 5 and mine was 15: there were about eighty numbers on the exchange. This exchange was in the post office, a large upright switchboard which stood with its back to the window: and it was served by the office clerks who would see a light go on, and go and attend to it when they had finished with the customer they were serving. By the time I had come there was a regular telephonist, who sat up against this exchange perched up in the window, so that her legs made quite a shop window display on occasions. Public telephone boxes were just being installed, and the old doctor was very angry about them: 'You see, my boy, they'll just drop in twopence and expect the doctor to pop up like that.' And in the event he was not far wrong: but at first the telephone was not used much for communication with the doctor, and most of the requests for visits were by laboriously written messages or sometimes by a relative coming into the surgery. The messages could be very difficult to decipher, and often gave little information beyond the name of the person writing it — the doctor was expected to be quite omniscient.

Dr Tench told me of a man whose wife was going to have a baby at High Easter. He had told them to send for him when she was ready, and as he was driving his trap into High Easter one day he met this man walking towards Dunmow, and who touched his hat and walked on. Some hours later when Dr Tench got home to tea and to make up the medicines after the round, he found a message from this man to say that his wife was in labour and would he please come. He went out there again, and found that the baby had arrived quite a time before, and he said to the man:

'Didn't I see you walking into Dunmow? Couldn't you have told me then?'

The man replied:

'Doctor said, when my wife was ready, to come into Dunmow and tell him and that's what I done.'

The prevalent illnesses differed in many ways from those which we meet today. Broadly, they were due to poverty and deficiency, where nowadays they are more likely to be caused by affluence and excess. The old people, and parents and children in large families, tended to be short of food, badly clothed, and poorly housed in damp old cottages with no drains. It was all very picturesque in summertime, roses and honeysuckle round the door and thatch on the roof — but the artists who drew these cottages for the Christmas calendars did not see the dripping leaks and the rat infested walls, the weeds and the litter in the cold winter months. There was one of these isolated cottages which has now been demolished, and which I had to visit on my first Christmas Day. Old Dr Tench had died on the night before, so a kind friend asked me to share his Christmas lunch with his growing family: and it was from that cheerful atmosphere that I went out in the cold snowy afternoon as dusk came on. It was a long low thatched cottage with a

4

brick path round it, and when I knocked on the door a little girl of about eight came and let me in. Her entire clothing was a cut down shirt of her father's, and I remember her blue little feet on the cold snow-dusted brick. In the downstairs room there were several children huddled round the table on which there was the end of a loaf, a jam pot and a pot of tea. I was taken upstairs to the tiny bedroom, where the mother lay in bed with her latest child of a week old, she told me she was suffering from 'milk fever'; by her side was her husband desperately ill with pneumonia, and there was a small fire in the grate from which the children had been sent downstairs when I came up.

As I was going out I asked the little girl what she had had to eat that day, and she said: 'Oh, just bread and jam.'

It is nice to think that that family not only survived, but the girls were attractive, married well and made good wives, and gave their elderly parents an extremely comfortable old age.

I have another memory of that first Christmas in 1930 in the small country community I have described, where much real poverty existed. Charity is a word that is not liked nowadays, but most of what I saw was spontaneous and Christian. Many of the well-to-do regarded it as a duty to old servants or tenants or neighbours, especially at Christmas time, when it was the custom to take round Christmas parcels. These were made up carefully to match the wants of the families: food, clothing, sweets and even small toys.

Dr Tench was dying, but he had nurses in the house. The domestic work of the house was all done by servants, so that Mrs Tench and her sisters would spend long days making up these parcels for the doctor's poor patients who were either on the Parish, or in his dispensary. If they were reasonably near, the parcels would be strapped precariously on the carriers of their bicycles and they would wheel them out, stop for a chat and bicycle home.

But most of the poorer patients were in the villages round: old worn out labourers, widows, or large families on pitifully low wages or with a sick wage earner 'on the club'. These were my job, and my car was loaded up according to the routine round of the day. Mondays and Thursdays were out at High Easter where I ate a picnic lunch in the surgery, returning through the Rodings. Tuesdays and Fridays were out to Takeley, and sometimes Hatfield Broad Oak, with Felsted in the afternoons and sometimes Broxted and Thaxted as well.

A few of the parcels were enormously heavy and included a single huge lump of coal. The best coal was delivered in really large pieces, and it was the job of the gardener's boy to break these up to a reasonable size: but around Christmas time Mrs Tench would go down to the cellar with sticky labels and put the names of families on appropriate lumps, which were brought up and delivered by me. I grumbled at first but was ashamed when I saw the genuine gratitude in the cottages.

The majority of the older farm workers spoke very broad Essex. They would tell me that they had little or no schooling before they started work almost as children: it was quite a surprise to me when I started at very short notice because of Dr Tench's illness, to find not only that I knew nothing of the minor common complaints about which I was being consulted, but I could not understand in the least what my patients were talking about! The finest specimens of dialect were a fairly high sing song addressed to some piece of furniture well away from me, and in the third person with frequent references to 'doctor'. At first I thought they were referring to my predecessor, and it took me a little time before I realised that this was their polite way of addressing me personally. A number of their everyday words were strange to me, and the Reverend Edward Gepp (who was the vicar of High Easter for a time) compiled a dictionary of Essex terms, many of which are common East Anglian as well. A tissick was a cough, bangled was knocked about, to count meant to think, and to fare was to be or to seem: 'times I fare that giddy'; helped up meant muddled with, king was used when getting better: 'Oh, I'm king today doctor', mosey was not too good, passel a lot of: bindley meant weakly, and pray seemed sometimes to occur at every other word as a chorus or exclamation. If you asked a patient how he felt he might reply, 'Oh pray', usually to mean how bad he was: quite often it meant just 'go on' to the doctor; and us usually referred to the speaker himself.

The younger generation had usually been to school, and the teacher was no longer someone from the neighbourhood with the same dialect and expressions, but was what they

6

called 'college trained', in fact introducing a cockney accent which did not combine well with the original pure Essex. Finally broadcasting has levelled it all out now, except in the very old, but I was delighted just before I retired to find that I really couldn't understand what one old chap was trying to tell me.

I first went to Dunmow on a Saturday in July, sent by the medical Superintendent of St Mary's as the only member of the junior staff who had no commitment that day, because Dr Tench was ill and wanted an assistant who he hoped would stay and follow him.

I was met at the station by an elderly man in chauffeur's uniform and a very old fashioned motor car. Dr Tench had it built specially for him in 1927, a two seater cabriolet body on to a 16 h.p. Wolseley chassis. It was built by the London Carriage Company and he had designed it himself: it was lined with morocco leather, and the windows pulled up and down with a silk covered sash cord similar to the ones found in first class railway carriages then. The inside door handles and window fittings were apparently made of ivory. It had high pressure tyres with an extremely intricate method of changing the wheels, as the rims came off: and it had no front wheel brakes. I subsequently bought it for £32, and used it for my first two years, when it gave endless trouble. I finally sold it for £2/10/0, but I wish I had it now. I was driven to Rood End, a smart Georgian house right on the street with green shutters all beautifully painted and very spick and span. Inside was fumed oak furniture and masses of photographs covering the walls everywhere. They consisted of relations, tennis and cricket teams, and churches and clergymen to represent Mrs Tench's contribution. The mantelpieces were covered with baize runners with bobbles attached: and there was a great deal of silverplate dishes and dish-covers everywhere.

There was an elderly assistant, Dr Wills, who looked much older than he really was because he had a long biblical beard and a high pitched giggly laugh. He was a wealthy bachelor and only did medicine as a hobby: Dr Tench had installed him as the Resident Medical Officer at Felsted school and he lived with the unmarried masters. I later found out that he doctored the school outpatients in his sitting room, in which there was an enormous cupboard with a series of long drawers. Out of these drawers he used

7

to take dressings for wounds and septic spots and so on, and into the other end of the drawer he would put any bits of soiled dressings which he thought he could use again. The smell on opening the drawer was unbelievable.

He also had a folding scalpel which he used to keep in a waistcoat pocket along with a piece of cotton wool. Apparently this scalpel had four uses: he used to weed the masters' tennis court with it, he used to scrape out the ash from his pipe, he used to scrape the crust off impetigo, and he used to incise boils. After each time he used it he would wipe it with the piece of cotton wool, which he replaced in his pocket along with the knife.

He was now over in Dunmow trying to do the practice there until somebody like myself arrived. We had lunch at once, a course of fish and then a joint and then a pudding, and I found that this was the regulation meal twice a day and never varied. The cooking was ample and excellent, and at first I wondered where it all went to until one day I walked past the kitchen door which was ajar, and saw the staff of five with another half dozen friends and relations (including the police inspector) finishing off what had come out of the dining room.

Dr Wills announced after lunch that he would show me 'the arrangements of the house'; we went upstairs through a hall which had a tortoise stove in the middle and an iron pipe running right up through the ceiling and out through the roof: this he told me was the central heating. At the end of a long passage he took me into a vast bathroom, which had been a bedroom until three years before when a legacy to Mrs Tench had enabled her to install a bath for the first time in their thirty-seven years in Dunmow. Dr Wills told me that this room was for the ladies. We went downstairs through a baize door into the corridor leading to the kitchen, and off this was a lavatory with an enormous cistern over it. A pipe led up to it with a handle, and I was told that it was the work of the gardener's boy to pump the cistern full each morning; the water came from a well in the yard, and this room was for the maids of the house. Dr Wills then took me out through the garden door along a path round a curving brick wall covered with ivy until we finally arrived at a rickety door which he opened, and pointing to one of two wooden seats side by side said, 'That's mine'. This double seat was directly over the cess-pit into which the drains of the rest of the house ran, and outside the lavatory there were two huge flagstones. Every quarter two men arrived with a horse and 'night soil cart' which was backed up to the cess-pool, and they were given a pound and a bottle of gin to empty the cess-pit during the night.

The house was furnished with the standard arrangement of bells. Along the corridor outside the kitchen there was a row of bells on the end of spiral springs, each one pulled by a wire from the appropriate door or room, and with a number above it or a letter to identify it. As the house was built of lath and plaster there were rat runs from one end to the other and frequently the bells jangled a little bit as a rat trod on one of the wires. The front door had a brass bell-pull by the side of it with 'day bell' at the top and 'night bell' at the bottom, and I was intrigued by the fact that there was only one pull for both bells. The night bell was coiled right over the doctor's bed: and the solution was quite ingenious, for the wire to the day bell in the kitchen corridor had a spring on it half way along, which ran to the bell over the doctor's bed. This meant that an ordinary pull only disturbed the bell in the passage downstairs, but a hefty jerk would also disturb the one upstairs. Dr Tench then used to throw up the window and hold a consultation with the messenger on the pavement about the patient, and I followed this custom to start with, even getting my newly married wife to knit me a nightcap to make the part more realistic.

The consulting room and surgery were at the far end of the house down a long passage, and Dr Tench rarely used the back room, which I turned into my consulting room. When I arrived it was full of unopened journals, and the main piece of furniture in it was the empty case of an upright grand piano, in which he stored his instruments. The window opened on to the garden and just outside there was a row of yew trees and a rockery with ferns growing out of it. When we had been in the house for some time we decided to get rid of the rockery: when we took the first few top rocks away we found that it was a vast rubbish heap consisting mainly of medicine bottles many of which were broken, but all of which had evidently contained the specimens of urine which patients had brought to be tested, and which the doctor used to throw just straight out of the

9

window on to the rockery. There were also quite interesting geological strata corresponding with the domestic life of Dr Tench: at one level there would be fragments of small chamber pots and mugs from the nursery; at another level great masses of oyster shells and champagne bottles: but the specimen bottles were present throughout.

There was a remarkably fine tennis court for those days in a rather beautiful walled garden which sloped down to what was called the Doctor's Pond. It had that name from a Dr Luckin who had experimented on it with self-righting boats and he was reputed finally to have evolved the old fashioned life-boat with floats at either end. At one corner of the tennis court there was a tremendous white-flowering bridal creeper so called from its resemblance to a bridal veil. I suggested that it might interfere with the tennis, but old Mrs Tench looked very solemn and said I must on no account remove it. It was a screen to foil the view of two old ladies who lived up on the downs opposite, and who, in the afternoons when the doctor used to have a tennis party, used to train their telescope on to the court and the garden. The doctor had a great reputation with the ladies, and in the early days his wife often wondered how it was that his tennis partners were so rapidly known and discussed round the tea tables in the neighbourhood, until one day she spotted the two old ladies peering excitedly through their telescope at what was going on, and decided to block their view.

Dr Tench was a very sick man when I first started practise in Dunmow in October of 1930; as I have said, he died on Christmas Eve. He had intended to take on an assistant 'with a view' who would come and work with him for a year and then buy the practice from him.

When he was a young man Dr Tench had a severe bout of rheumatic fever which kept him in bed for several weeks. He recovered but he had mitral regurgitation which was well compensated, so much so that he was a distinguished cricketer and tennis player until his late fifties; then the compensation failed, and he became increasingly subject to attacks of breathlessness and heart failure. But when I arrived he still fully intended to show me in for the following year, although I could see at a glance that he had no hope of doing that; for he had already had acute shortness of breath on even the slightest exertion, and spent most of his time in bed or in a chair. He made a great effort and even proposed one day to came and pay a visit with me. We had only got a couple of miles before he had an acute attack of dyspnoea and I had to turn for home and give him oxygen. The only drugs there were for a failing heart were oxygen and digitalis, and it was the custom to give both morphine and atrophine at night and during acute attacks. He had a great belief in leeches, and I used to have to apply them to the bases of both lungs and get them off by covering them with a handful of salt before putting them back in their bowl for use next time. Towards the end he lapsed into delirium, and the nurse used to keep him quiet by giving him an empty medicine bottle with a cork in it, and a piece of wrapping paper which she put on the left side of the bed. With incredibly rapid movements he would wrap up the medicine bottle and fold it neatly and put it away on to the right side and lie still and content, while the nurse carefully unwrapped the bottle and put it back on the left hand side for him to do all over again when he roused. His wife told me that he had done this for so long that it was the one automatic motion that soothed him. I had to get up nearly every night to give him oxygen and morphia, and I was rather surprised to find that he was very afraid of dying. I can only remember one or two patients who showed this same terror because usually death seems to come easily and naturally to most people.

With one poor lady this fear of death was understandable. All her life she had been a rigid non-conformist, with an obsessional sense of guilt. She believed implicitly in the afterworld, and although her sins must have been of an extremely minor character, they loomed so large, and her image of God was such a stern and unforgiving one, that she was literally convinced that she was going into hell fire for eternity. I wished that some of the preachers who had been responsible for this had watched her desperate struggles to stay alive.

To return to Dr Tench. I used to spend quite a lot of time with him and he told me about himself: he intended to go up to Cambridge after public school (I think Haileybury) to join his elder brother there who was also going into medicine; but his rheumatic fever developed and kept him as an invalid for the next year or two during which he went

11

abroad to recover; afterwards going straight to the Middlesex Hospital.

At hospital Dr Tench was popular and successful; he worked well and carried off a number of prizes: he was the contemporary and close friend of John Bland Sutton and the consultants of that age group, and he held a number of house jobs, so that when he came down to practise in Dunmow he was as well equipped as any young doctor in those days. A post-graduate education was unknown; you learnt what there was of medicine and expected that to stand you in good stead for the rest of your life. He was quite prepared to do major operations on the kitchen table, giving the anaesthetic himself. His midwifery was up to date for 1890: and he used forceps adeptly but far too often. In fact when I looked at the page in the ledger devoted to confinements, the entries ran either 'born before delivery' or 'chloroform and forceps'.

The arrival of this handsome and athletic young doctor in the neighbourhood fluttered the dovecotes in this small country community, and every mama with an eligible daughter scraped an acquaintance with him: I think he had a good opinion of himself to start with, and his reception rather confirmed it. However he soon married the daughter of a local clergyman, who like many churchmen in those days was a cultured man with a university degree. Religion played a much more important part in people's lives than it does now, and most of the village or small town attended church or chapel at least once on Sundays. The clergyman was an important figure in the community and exercised considerable authority. Church livings provided a gentleman's income, besides which many parsons had private means.

Attendance at church was not only for worship. It was a time and place for meeting of friends, for showing off hats and dresses, and for young people to look each other over, and to manoeuvre for introductions. Hence much of the social life centred round the rectories and vicarages, for with very limited horse transport, entertainment and recreation had to be much in the neighbourhood. Tennis and croquet parties, tea and 'at homes', musical evenings and amateur dramatics were where young people met and fell in love and got engaged. In Dr Tench's case I was told that it was a hard frost and a moonlight skating party on the rectory lake that set the scene for his proposal.

He was gay and gregarious and above all very kind and sympathetic. He took a great deal of trouble over his patients and never minded being interrupted or called out at odd hours. He appeared to me to be very old fashioned and out of date, but he was still a very good doctor, experienced and shrewd and above all he knew when a patient was ill. He was much loved, and had a very large circle of friends. At his funeral the quite large Dunmow church was completely crowded out.

CHAPTER II

COUNTRY TOWN AND COUNTRY PEOPLE

Fifty years ago in 1930 when I first settled in practice Dunmow was a small market town between Braintree and Bishop's Stortford to the east and west, and Saffron Walden and Chelmsford to the north and south. It was sufficiently far from any of them to be a centre to the small community around; it had a market on Tuesdays, and in the past it had had a charter and a corporation. The little single line railway had brought it into closer touch with the outside world, but in the main it was still a definite unit on which the surrounding countryside relied. The only industry was farming, and the farm workers and their wives would come into Dunmow to do their shopping, where most of their needs were catered for by small town shops and craftsmen who now belong to a vanished tradition.

The first that comes to my mind was the harness maker's shop, Savill's. Savill was a tall imposing gentleman with white hair and a saddler's apron; his assistant, Harris was small and short and bald with a moustache, and later on became my part-time groom. Savill's shop was in the wide Market Hill, which ran off the High Street at the market cross for about 100 yards before narrowing right down to North Street. A large glass window had shelves right along it which were crowded with every sort of leather and harness, and were in fact simply the shelves on which Savill kept his enormous stock of materials and tools of his trade for working inside. If I took a piece of harness to be repaired or renewed, he would look at it and scratch his head and mutter 'Yes, I've got something somewhere which will do that job', and he would hunt along the shelves until he found it. I used to be fascinated, because every here and there would be some object which I could not identify and we would spend a long time as he explained it; and that would lead on to other items, until finally we had to remind ourselves what it was that he was originally hunting for. One day he rediscovered some of the plumes from the ceremonial harness of Lady Warwick's horses and presented me with one in its silver mount. He was a pillar of the non-conformist chapel, which may have accounted for his slow, deliberate and impressive speech.

Roper the chemist in the High Street comes next, a very important person when I first started practising, as he was a tower of strength while I slowly made a fumbling acquaintance with the common ailments of the farming community. Chemists in those days were often consulted before the doctor for minor ailments, and they had a vast store of practical knowledge. I had to beware when patients came to me because often they would only take that step when the chemist had failed: they were often unwilling to admit that they had tried it, so I had to be careful not to prescribe something which they would already have found useless. Roper was an oldish man and looked on me as still wet behind the ears: I suppose he had been there for forty years when I arrived, and he was quite renowned as the drawer of teeth, as the dentist only came once a week and charged far too much for the pockets of farm workers, who only earned 28/- a week and often had large families. Like Savill's, his shop was an enchanting Aladdin's cave of every kind of medicine and appliance, all mixed in with his toothbrushes and sponges, pills for dogs and powders for fleas. The walls were lined with beautiful wooden drawers with yellow glass handles, and in the window there were two huge display jars one with green and one with red fluid inside. Until I had a secretary, Daphne, my wife, helped me with the practice accounts. Roper wouldn't send in a bill, although I bought a lot of drugs and dressings through him. It was only when she had a real row with him at the end of two years that we finally got sheets and sheets of bills, much of which I had quite forgotten. Dr Tench only sent his bills out at the end of the year, often six months after that, and Roper expected to do the same, as did several other tradesmen.

A few doors along was Wood the tailor. He also was an ardent non-conformist. Small and dapper with white hair smoothed to one side, he would work perched up cross-legged on a counter. In time his son took the same position: in fact he suffered from a weakness in his legs which made that position a much easier one to work in. Wood made some breeches for me, apologising for having to charge £2.0.0. He told me that when he had started — I suppose forty or fifty years before — the charge for a pair of breeches was 7/6d. The very best with special leather strappings were half a guinea, and he said: 'You know,

15

Doctor, I had to make them good. I saw them every day of my life, and couldn't bear to see a badly fitting pair.' His cutter was an old lady called Mrs Ashard, who lived with her husband in a little house long pulled down now, which was in a small courtyard behind Market Hill, alongside the old Town Hall, approached through a dark little passage through a block of houses. She had a chronic varicose ulcer, and I saw a good deal of her. One day she looked at my breeches and said: 'When that pair wears out doctor, let me have them to copy. You buy the cloth and I will do it for nothing.' They must have lasted me between twenty and thirty years. Her son was the shoemaker down North Street in a little shop so small that only two, or at the most three, people could crowd in at once in front of his long bench where he and his apprentice were working in full view of the customers. He was born lame but was always cheerful, and he was a marvellous craftsman; every repair was a work of art and lasted twice as long as usual.

Next door to Ashard there was a yard and then the old town lock-up, a dark little den with tiny high-barred windows and then a pleasant small Georgian house with a board above the front door saying Scrivener, locksmith, in elaborate scroll writing. Here Miss Scrivener mended cane chairs, upholstered easy chairs and made loose covers. She did beautiful work and took great pride in it; she gave me the feeling that she would mend a chair as a favour and payment was only a secondary consideration.

Back up Market Hill was Lewis the ironmonger's. When I first knew it, it belonged to Lewis father, a rather uncertain-tempered gentleman who dyed his hair. In time he decided to let it grow and the result was a most surprising skewbald wig of white and ginger. His shop was much of a piece with the saddler opposite, with large wooden counters and drawers right up to the ceiling. Brushes and brooms and pans hung from the ceiling in rows and oil lamps and stoves were piled in great mounds along with every kind of pot and pan and kettle and tray. If there was a crowd in the shop and somebody got pushed out of the narrow gangway, there would be an enormous crash of falling ironmongery mingled with the clatter of broken glass. One had to be very careful about turning round, and a small child could be lethal. Old Lewis and his assistant knew what every drawer held: you only had to ask for a particular size of nail or screw, hook or door handle and he would unerringly select one of the great battery of drawers and produce it. As he grew old his sons took on, fat Lewis and thin Lewis. They had had a serious row sometime earlier, and never spoke to each other except on business in the shop. Long ago the old father would tell me fascinating stories of when Lady Warwick had one of her grand shoots at Easton Lodge for Edward, Prince of Wales, before the turn of the century. Lewis used to provide the Lodge with all the cartridges for the guns, and he and his father used to sit for nights on end beforehand loading the cartridges by hand with their machine. He said that sometimes the order came for several thousand with only a week to execute it.

Next door was Luckin the grocer. It was a real old-fashioned grocer's shop, again with wooden counters and jars and a beautiful bacon-cutting machine, and the children when they were small were often given a treat of being hoisted onto the counter and winding the handle for the family's rashers. In the window was a coffee machine which used to run most of the day, and gave off the lovely smell of grinding and roasting coffee. The shop was run by two brothers, one in the shop, the other in the background doing the books. Like the Lewises, it was a strictly business arrangement, without family affection. Luckin had a rather lovely little house between the shop and our home, Rood End, and in the enclosed garden, in the middle of the grass, there was a stile with a thatched cover over it. The story was that this was the stile where Luckin had proposed to his wife, and one summer when they went away for a holiday, he arranged a great surprise for her when she came home. He had privately bought the stile from the farmer and had arranged for it to be installed during the two or three weeks that they were away. The house itself was spotless and was a lovely Georgian house with very little alterations. The walls were either panelled or painted, the rooms furnished with good antique furniture, and rather cluttered with brass, but even this was of a very high quality and almost unobtainable nowadays; there were some beautiful horse brasses on their original leather swags.

Lucking the butcher, a few doors away from us, had a shop which was also part of the row of Georgian houses. It was a large room with marble slabs all round, and joints hanging from the beams overhead. There was always clean, fresh sawdust on the floor, but the shop was nearly filled by the presence of the great Mr Lucking himself, a huge man with a striped blue and white butcher's apron. He had a brother who did the dirty work, who was as lean as he was fat. He wore an old shapeless cap and his face had a twisted expression with no teeth. The butchers killed their own beasts on the premises, and every so often the main road from Bishop's Stortford to Colchester would be blocked off by a lorry backed up against the entrance to Lucking's yard, while bullocks were unloaded. There was always a considerable gap over the pavement between the back of the lorry and the yard, and it was quite a frequent occurrence for one of the bullocks to jump over or knock down the hurdles which were held up to guide them in, and then there would be a grand chase right along the High Street and all the traffic had to wait.

My favourite was Stock the blacksmith. He was about fifty when I first took a horse there to be shod and he was nearly eighty when I last saw him. He was a faithful friend and a marvellous smith, and knew more about horses' legs and feet than most vets. Captain Blyth from Braintree had a great respect for his opinion; if a horse was lame and Blyth came out, he would ask to have Stock there as well to take off a shoe if necesssary and cut down the hoof to look for pus, if he thought there was any there. Stock was usually right.

I suppose all smithies are much the same, but this was as typical as any. It was roofed over entirely with glass like a greenhouse, with a huge forge in the middle with enormous bellows, and although it was a large room it was crammed with discarded horseshoes, and all sorts of agricultural instruments and tools, either broken and discarded or for repair. There was a great long workbench with lathes and drills on it, and he himself was a huge man with a slow deliberate manner and the kindest nature imaginable. A horse which was nervous or difficult to begin with soon settled under his soothing murmur, and he never had trouble with one of mine. I would take the horses up to be shod, and they always loved turning into his narrow yard which led to the smithy. Outside there would always be a number of blackbirds and tits and finches waiting for crumbs, for he loved his birds and fed them regularly; usually there were one or two blackbirds hopping around

18

the floor of the forge, in and out among the horses' feet and sometimes perching on Stock's back as he bent to put on a shoe. He used to grumble gently when they left a mess there.

The children remember Dolly Dowsett's sweet and toy shop up at the further end of the town. Like so many of the shops it was crowded and crammed with half-forgotten toys, but Dolly was a solid slow worker, and patience would nearly always produce what a child wanted. She would clamber up to shelves high up in the ceiling and take down inumerable parcels before she found the right one, but on the way up she opened most exciting packages. A visit to Dolly's meant a long session.

Also very important in the children's lives was another shop kept by two little ladies whose real name I never knew because they were always called the Misses Tiggywinkle. This was a tiny little shop by the Saracen's Head with steep steps up to it; it was a confectioners and they used to make the most delicious jam puffs which the children's cousin Tim always made a beeline for every time he came to stay.

There were three bakers in the town. Child lived in a small house up New Street, the front having been changed into a tiny shop, leading through to the back premises where the baking went on. He produced the most wonderful stoneground wholemeal bread in round crusty loaves, which he delivered on a bicycle with an enormous basket specially constructed to drop into a frame connected with his handlebars. The children and I would tend to skin the loaf, cutting the crust off all round until finally there was only a lump of dough left in the middle. The other two bakers were more professional and delivered by van. Poney and Wilson next door to the Doctor's pond was a big baker who at Christmas used to take the turkeys off half the small town and tie a label on them and put them into his oven, because few of us had ovens that could accommodate a 18 lb turkey. On Christmas Day I would take ours down early, and then go to the Saracen's Head and borrow from them their huge pewter hot water carving dish with a cover to match. At lunchtime I would go down to collect the turkey, but Wilson always had a tumbler full of neat whisky which he expected me to down before I could take the turkey home. He thought that my excuse that I was on duty and might have to go out to a case was pretty feeble.

Legg was the other baker, in a Georgian house beyond: his shop was on the corner, but when I went in to see any of the family as a patient I went in at the front door which was by the side and had to run the gauntlet of the extremely fierce-looking bulldog. In fact it was a bitch with the sweetest disposition, who accepted me as a long-lost friend, but I am told by people who showed fear of it that it reacted accordingly and went for them. The Legg family were exactly like playing cards of Happy Families — the little baker with spectacles, and his enormous wife and daughter.

Sams the milkman was a well-known figure around the town, with his hand churn mounted on two huge wheels. It was very unhygienic, and all the milk that came into our household used to be boiled before it was given to the children. Like most of the tradespeople he was a very friendly character, and always had a kind word for the children.

The cars were looked after by a branch of Salmon, the bicycle shop. They had a workshop behind the main premises, where they would service the cars, mend punctures and so on, but for anything major the car had to go to Chelmsford. In fact the brother who used to look after our cars was a very good mechanic and could do most things if he had the tools. He came up every morning with a boy wheeling a long trolley loaded with two gallon petrol cans, and he would fill up the tanks and leave two cans as spares, and come next day to replenish them again. At the same time he also checked both water and oil.

Living in the town was in many ways very different from living in a farming community. Quite a large number of the older people could neither write nor read, and their lives had been simple ones of hard work with few interruptions from the outside world. During the first world war a number of men had gone into the army, but very many of them had remained behind as essential farm workers. Buses had only recently started to run very occasionally through the villages, usually on market days and on Saturdays only. It was this farming community which made up the bulk of the practice which I had taken over; it was a very static community, and differed a great deal from the changing population which many of my friends encountered. This meant that there was a very happy continuity between the doctor and patients' families which went on for several generations at a time, and gave one a beautiful picture of what the middle generation looked like when they were young, and what they might develop into when they were old. In addition the doctor rapidly became one of the community. It was not just a professional contact which ceased outside the consulting room or the patient's home, and it must be remembered that doctors paid a great many more visits to the homes of their patients, partly because the latter had no transport: but especially because it was expected, and it gave us invaluable information about the environment in which the illness developed. One could assess the poverty, overcrowding, the stairs for the arthritic, the distant outside toilet for the elderly bronchitic or ailing heart, and at any rate try to do something about it. Apart from this, nursing was much more important in the management of illness for which we had no specific drugs, and the doctor had to see the home and advise the housewife how to make the best of the limited resources he found there. Diet was always seriously considered and restraint had to be used tactfully for the widespread belief that 'you had to keep the patient's strength up'. I remember clambering up a steep and rickety stairway into the roof of a cottage on a sweltering summer afternoon to see a young labourer bathed in perspiration with a temperature of 106° after three to four days of lobar pneumonia. His sister downstairs had told me he was a bit off his food, I found him struggling valiantly with half a rabbit, a mound of vegetables and three rounds of suet roll. But these were the people I was meeting in ordinary life, and the same applied to the shopkeepers and the postman and the dustman and the farmers themselves and all one's friends, the majority of whom were involved in this type of country life in one way and another. 'Daily breaders' had only just begun to settle in the neighbourhood, and they tended to be of the type who didn't have to get into their offices very early and who managed to leave before the rush hour. My old chief in hospital had advised me 'never make friends with your patients or patients of your friends': I soon realised that if I followed his advice I would have either no patients or no friends, and from the time that my wife and I settled down we were met with nothing but kindness and friendliness which has developed over the years into a deep bond: though of course there have been exceptions. At the same

21

time the old East Anglian attitude to 'foreigners' is still there, as I realised recently when I was in a shooting party of farmers and one said to me 'Let's see, doctor, you've been here quite a time now, haven't you?' I replied that it was around forty years, whereupon he said, 'Ah, yes, but you're still a foreigner, though your children are Essex born and bred.'

These then are the country men and women about whom I have these stories to tell, some sad and some gay, but all with real affection. One day I counted up the ages of six couples I was visiting: they combined to come to just over one thousand. Several of these men would put on smocks for their Sunday best, and I always regret that I did not take photographs of them. They usually shaved their upper lip and chin but left a fine line of whisker running down in front of their ears the whole way round. They had remarkably fine faces and tanned complexions and clear blue eyes, but nearly all of them were crippled with rheumatism as they got older; in fact rheumatism was the occupational disease of this part of the world. These men's bodies had been constantly subjected to strains and injuries from carrying heavy weights over uneven ground for long periods in bad weather. All their weight-bearing joints had been damaged in some way over the years, so that the 'bent countryman' was a natural description of the old labourer.

About half the farms still used horses for ploughing and reaping, and this certainly had a good deal to do with the character then of the farm workers. Each man had his own team of horses which he looked after and worked himself: naturally they developed a close bond together, and the horses were unlikely to work as well with an unfamiliar voice and hand. The majority of the horses were Suffolk Punches, fine chestnut animals: and I have seen fourteen of them working in two adjacent fields in teams of two and three, a magnificent sight. At harvest time horses, men and often women all helped; the corn was first cut and bound into stooks, which were later collected on farm wagons and taken to the threshing yard. Here travelling teams of steam threshers would come in turn and work at each farm. Combine harvesters did not appear until after the war and even then were usually owned and hired out by large firms: and it was unusual for the smaller farms to buy one independently. This close involvement between the farm worker, the horses and cattle that were his responsibility, and the land on which he worked so intimately, were what made him a unique and most attractive personality, and these people were the majority of my patients.

One old man used to come and see me regularly, and always performed the same ritual. He would produce a large paper bag out of which he took a number of apples, pears, vegetables or eggs, and laid them in a long line all round my consulting room desk. Having done that, he would sit down and say, 'Now, master, we can talk.' His complaint was of a worm which he said lived in his umbilicus and which roamed around just under his skin in the small hours of the morning. He was quite sure that if he pinched it in the right place he would be able to nip its head off, and his stomach wall was covered with scratches and bruises. He very rarely washed himself, but I doubt whether that was the cause of the irritation: I did my best for it, but I never managed to kill that worm of his.

A friend of mine took over a large farm in the mid-thirties. The old owner had died with no children, so that this young man came in as a stranger: but he kept on the old workers and did his best not to introduce new ways too quickly. I do not know whether the Essex farm worker is more suspicious of change than his counterparts elsewhere, but even as a doctor I found I had to go very slowly in putting my own ideas into practice rather than following the pattern of my old predecessor.

The young farmer settled down, but he told me that when the agricultural wage was raised early in the war, he paid his men one Saturday, putting the new rate into their envelopes. They all went away except two old men who hung about, and he finally went up to them and asked if anything was the matter.

'It's our wage packets, master.'

'Well, aren't they all right now? I've put in the new rate for you.'

'That's just it, master. We don't hold with our wages being mucked about without consulting we.'

Another example of the independence of the farm workers was when a stockman had been knocked down and badly bruised by a young bullock in the yard. He cracked some ribs and was in considerable pain, and after I had strapped him up I told him he would have to lie up for a day or two.

'I can't do that, doctor, who's going to look after my stock?'

'Isn't there anyone else who can do them for you?'

'No, doctor, they're my cattle and I have to look after them.'

'But they aren't your cattle; they belong to Mr R— and it's up to him to find someone else while you're sick.'

'Oh him — well I reckon he buys 'em and sells 'em, but they're my cattle and that's why I have to look after them.'

In any practice it is a very common thing for a girl to come and ask if she is pregnant. Sometimes she will not come to the point right away, but the question of the last period comes into every routine examination and it is a relief to the girl to be able to say what has really brought her. On the other hand the mothers would sometimes come with their daughters asking in a quite cheerful way if the girl was pregnant: and seemed pleased if one could say yes. They went away and made arrangements for the wedding to take place quite soon.

I said to one of the local parsons 'It seems a pity that you never have to marry girls who have not already become pregnant' and he replied, 'Young man, you know nothing. When a young couple wants to marry, they have got to know that they can have children, otherwise what is going to happen to them as they grow older? Our people rely on family life, they have to work hard to bring their children up, but they expect those children to look after them as they grow older and when they are past work. Otherwise it is the workhouse, even separation of husband from wife with only a meeting ceremoniously on Sundays. I won't say that some of these young women don't trap the young men that way!'

One family in the same village followed the oldest profession. Mother and daughter were quite inconceivably ugly, but they appeared to satisfy their clients. In due course the younger of the two produced a daughter and there were three Miss H. living in the same cottage. She in turn became pregnant: when to the horror of her mother and her grandmother and the astonishment of the whole village she announced that she was going to marry the man and in due course provided him with seven children. She was always looked upon as having let her family down.

For many years I looked after one old maiden lady who lived with her brother. When she was over seventy she became ill, and I went to see her one Monday and she told me that she had had a lovely weekend. Four of her grandchildren had come over to see her. I looked puzzled, and said that I had always thought she was unmarried whereupon she chuckled and said, 'Well, that doesn't stop me having a jolly good family and quite a number of grandchildren. You see, I never could marry my man but he was very good to me. When I was carrying my first I used to sing in the choir. And the vicar's sister, who kept house for him, once said to me, "Nellie, aren't you ashamed to come and worship in God's house in your condition? I should have thought all you could do was to fall down on your knees and ask him to forgive your sin." So I said to her, "Miss C., you're talking about sins. Have you ever heard of the sin of envy?"'

Soon after we were married I was driving slowly through the town with my wife when an old lady bowed to me and I waved back to her. When I said to my wife, 'She's got her nightie on' she squeaked with delight and disbelief, so I had to explain that the custom with farm workers was to have a bath on Saturday night and a complete change of clothing. They would put on their pants and vests and shirt, or vests and drawers and petticoat, and then a clean pair of pyjamas or nightgown, and so to bed. Next morning they would add to this the visible suit or dress which we were accustomed to see. So that when I asked one of my women patients to undress to examine her, she would peel off her clothes including the nightgown and so down to her chest or abdomen.

It reminded me of when I was first a house surgeon at the Paddington Green Children's Hospital. It was winter time, and a small baby was brought in, which I told the mother I would like to examine. I had to explain that this meant taking off all the child's clothes, and she said, 'Oh dear, doctor, it's going to be difficult. Last week I sewed him in for the winter.'

A wealthy bachelor was the subject of a large number of anecdotes, some of them true and some of them undoubtedly exaggerated, but his main characteristic was that he did exactly what he liked and he had plenty of money to do it with. Soon after I arrived I began to look after his mother who was in the last stages of one of the illnesses of old age, and she died not long afterwards leaving a large fortune to her son. He had been an athlete of international qualification in his youth, and he inherited a very large business up in the North where he spent a good deal of his time, but he kept his mother's hobby, which was racing. He had a very shrewd knowledge of horses and was so well-known on race courses that the bookies tended to shorten their odds as soon as they saw him coming. He betted in large amounts and on one occasion when he was picked up drunk in Bishop's Stortford because his Bentley was in the front garden of a house and he was fast asleep underneath it, the police brought as part of their evidence the fact that he had no knowledge at all of what money was in his pocket, although it amounted to several hundred pounds. His explanation in the magistrate's court next day was that he had been to Newmarket and had done quite well, and he thought it quite reasonable to say that he had in fact done rather better than usual: he thought it was several hundred pounds, but he said of course it might be more, even four figures.

I had a number of calls in the early hours of the morning to go out to him in a police court, because he boasted that in the whole of his life he had never gone to bed sober or without a woman if he had wanted one.

On one occasion he elected to go for trial at the assizes in Hertford and briefed an eminent counsel. The police surgeon based his evidence on a number of tests and observations at the police station where I had been present at the patient's request. Those were the days before blood or urine tests, so that the evidence was largely on the behaviour of the accused at the time of examination by the doctor. The surgeon said that his speech was almost unintelligible, that his tongue was very furred and that his breath was foul, and that his eyes were bloodshot and that the pupils did not respond to light. The defence counsel put my patient into the box and proceeded to examine him, but the presiding judge had constantly to stop the accused and ask him to speak more loudly and more plainly because nobody could understand what he was saying. Finally counsel asked him whether there was anything unusual with his speech that day, and he replied that that was in fact the way that he always talked, so that the police surgeon had only observed his ordinary manner. Counsel then invited the jury to look more closely at my patient, and with their permission he brought him up in front of them and asked him to open his mouth and put his tongue out. There was a gasp of horror at the furred white mass and the odour that came from it. Counsel then put a finger to pull down his lower eye-lid and show his bloodshot eye, at the same time turning to the jury and inviting them to examine each others' tongues and eyes. He had little difficulty in persuading them that if this was a test for drunkenness, they all stood in considerable peril on driving away from the court.

His estate in Essex was a large farm with a very good shoot on it, and I was one who was frequently invited there. The custom was to shoot until about three o'clock in the afternoon when we adjourned for lunch, and this is no bad idea in the ordinary way: except that in this particular case the lunch went on until about 5 p.m. and a good deal was drunk. My patient was no good with a gun, and he usually fortified himself both beforehand and during the day from a flask. He often wandered back to the house by himself, so that nobody took much notice when he did not turn up at the later drives. On one occasion however he had left early as usual, but when we gathered for lunch he did not appear and inquiry showed he had not returned to the house. A search party was sent out and he was found fast asleep in a ditch with his gun between his knees, loaded and with the 'safe' off.

His nephew has written: 'He has left behind him many happy and affectionate memories, and knowing many of his old staff both here in Essex and in the North, I can vouch for their regard and devotion, some of them having been with him all their lives. Your anecdotes are quite typical and I recall many which I can record at first hand.

'Once I took him to Newmarket to a meeting attended by Royalty, at a time when he had been subject to considerable correspondence relating to surtax, marked of course O.H.M.S. This always upset him and during the afternoon he suddenly made to leave the Members' Bar; I asked him where he was going and he replied "to the Royal Enclosure to ask the Queen to stop writing to him, otherwise he would tell the Duke of Edinburgh".'

Another story concerned a proposed visit to the South of

France with one of his lady-friends; she had been rather quiet and when pressed said that being considerably younger she was worried about the future, when he would no long be there; she felt that in addition to meeting as he did the not inconsiderable expenses attendant upon their style of holiday-making, it would be very nice if she could be given a sum, both to remember their happy days together and ensure that the future could be lived in a style to which she had become increasingly attracted. Uncle George replied that he had also been doing some thinking and had decided that as he was no longer as young as he used to be, together with the general increase in the cost of living, he would increase his stud-fee to five hundred guineas!

He finally became senile, and slowly sank into coma and death, but at no point did he appear to be anxious or unhappy about his future in the next world.

Small towns and villages in Essex still had a social order which was Victorian when I first came to Dunmow. A few prominent people had a great influence on the general public; one or two landowners with large houses owned many of the farms, and as landlords had to be respected. They were usually J.P.s and active on administrative committees such as the County Council: there was a strong Church with a clergyman who usually had a university degree, a school master who was respected, and then a number of prominent farmers and well-to-do professional men, the doctor and the solicitor: and finally prosperous business men — corn merchants, brewers and old established shop-keepers. The opinions and behaviour of these people were carefully noticed and discussed by the public, and exerted considerable influence: and that of the clergymen was probably as important as any, for the churches were still well attended, and the vicarage or rectory was a centre of both social and parish activities.

We were fortunate in our clergymen in the neighbourhood, and I can think of half a dozen who were men of considerable standing; on the other hand several of them were eccentric, but all were very kind to me when I first came as a young doctor.

In Dunmow there was a Reverend Noel Mellish, V.C., kindly and absentminded, to the point of forgetting his false teeth sometimes when he went in to take the service, and his wife was known to beat a hurried retreat to the vicarage and bring them up to his stall for him to continue the service. He had won his V.C. in the trenches in France when he went out to minister to the wounded in no-man's land with no thought for his own safety. He is reputed to have done it in his own absentminded way, hardly noticing that a battle was going on, so intent was he on his duty as a Minister of God.

In Great Easton there lived the retired Rector Mr Capel, a strong and unusual character. He was ninety when I arrived and I looked after him until his death three years later.

The first time I came to see him he called out, 'Boy, do you drink beer?' I thought it polite to say that I did, whereupon he shouted to his wife to bring beer for the doctor, and he would not speak until I had downed a pint. This was the custom from then on, whether I really wanted it or not.

His mother was a Maynard from Easton Lodge and he had originally gone into the Navy where he had a good allowance, and was able to keep a yacht with several paid hands. He was a very good boxer, and I believe had been heavy-weight champion of the Navy at one point. His career came to an abrupt end when he fell in love and wanted to marry the daughter of a Judge. She was about to enter a convent but she agreed to marry him only if he entered the Church. So he left the Navy and attended theological college and became a curate at Bristol where they were married: then he asked for and was granted the living of Great Easton in the gift of Lady Warwick. He still kept up his boxing and I have been told that soon after he came to the parish, the blacksmith at Thaxted announced in the local pub that he had heard there was a clergyman chap come to the neighbourhood who thought he could use his fists, and that he'd be pleased to teach him a lesson if he cared.

The Reverend Capel arrived on his bicycle within a day or two, and suggested that they should have a fight in the churchyard the next Sunday before Matins. If the Rector won, the blacksmith was to attend the service, but if the blacksmith won, then the Rector would go over and do a day's work at his forge on the following day. The story goes that the Rector won handsomely; they remained great friends, and the boxing match in the churchyard before Matins was repeated from time to time.

Mr Vincent of High Easter was a bachelor, who lived with a grumpy sister in a gloomy vicarage which is now a block of flats. It was tumbledown and dirty, and there was only one really comfortable room which was Mr Vincent's study, which he never allowed his sister to enter under any circumstances. The walls were lined with books; there were a couple of vast sofas and several armchairs, mostly inhabited by gun-dogs; there was an enormous fire, and the room was lit by a large oil lamp which did its best to penetrate the thick fog of tobacco smoke which always seemed to be there. He was a very fine shot, and he always wore his clerical collar out shooting. He was much in demand as he could be relied on to fill the bag: in those days the stubble was long and left on into November or December, so that it was partridge country still, and I have watched him take a number of right-and-lefts in succession with almost insolent ease.

Much later during the war I sometimes met him at lunch at the Saracen's Head when my wife was away with the children: he had become very deaf. Food was scarce, and so were waitresses, so that we all sat at a long table and ate whatever the manager could scrape together. The day the vicar and I sat together we were having rabbit, and when it came to his turn a plate was put in front of him with seven rabbit heads on it. He looked surprised, but made no comment, helped himself to vegetables and set to as best he could. A few minutes later the little waitress came and whispered something in his ear and started to take his plate away.

'I haven't finished yet,' he said and seized his plate and put it down in front of him.

The girl whispered in his ear again and once more tried to take it away and again he took the plate from her, put it down and said:

'In a minute, I've not finished yet.'

The girl once more bent down, but this time instead of whispering she bellowed in his ear:

'It's the DOG'S dinner.'

Another eccentric bachelor lived by himself, and he is reputed to have had curious feeding habits. As the local

30

parson he was invited out to dinner a good deal, and he had a waterproof poacher's pocket in his dinner jacket, into which he used to shovel any second helping he could get hold of. When he got home he would tip this into a tin and label it with his host's name and the date: later in the week he would inspect his larder and say, 'Ah, that was the pheasant followed by apple tart. Splendid, I'll just warm it all up, and that'll do me this evening.'

The Reverend John Maryon Wilson was also a bachelor rector, a 'squarson' who was a considerable farmer, and who hunted regularly. Like Mr Capel he had been a notable boxer in his time, and had also been to university. I was told a story by one of his friends. They were two young men riding home after a day with the Essex Deer Hounds: they took a short cut and came to a farm chase which belonged to a man who was anti-hunting, and who disapproved of riders using his farm yard as a thoroughfare. He had pulled a sheep hurdle across the gateway, and had stood in the middle of this telling them to go round the long way. Mr Wilson said to his friend, 'What do you think, shall we?' the reply was yes, so they kicked their horses' ribs, and jumped the hurdle one on each side of the farmer, and disappeared through his yard.

At Great Easton both Canon Widdrington and his wife were great characters, and close friends of ours, until he retired and they left the neighbourhood. He was a very impressive looking man, and it was quite a sight to see him on a winter's day in his cassock and beret and gumboots, walking through the snow to carry Communion to one of his parishioners. While he was at Oxford he had been one of the original members of the Fabian Society with Sidney Webb and his wife, and I believe Bernard Shaw: he was a highly cultured man and his house was full of books and paintings, but it was gloriously untidy and nothing was ever thrown away. At one time the bathroom was used as a wine cellar and one had to steer down a narrow path from the door to the basin with empty and full bottles on either side.

He was a great gourmet, and his wife was an excellent cook. My wife and I were once asked out to lunch on a Thursday, to meet their old doctor from Newport who was just retiring: and I thought I could manage it fairly comfortably although I had the round at High Easter in the afternoon where I usually started off at 2 o'clock. We were told that we were to eat one of their home-reared geese, and it was to be quite an occasion. When we arrived we were given a menu which was beautifully written out in French in the pale faded ink and the flowing handwriting of the restaurants of the Mediterranean. It was on large headed paper, with the name of a small bistro at Sète near Montpellier, and the usual little highly coloured decorations on each side. In fact this was one of the menus that Mrs Widdrington used to write out during August regularly every day, when she and the Rector used to go down and stay in this small inn: some of the time the patron and his wife would go off on their holiday and visit their family, and Mr and Mrs Widdrington would take on the care of the pub. Her cooking was up to the occasion, and I can imagine nothing more at home than himself behind the bar in a pair of jeans and a T-shirt and of course the inevitable beret. In the afternoons he used to swim gently round the bay, making skilful use of the local currents to bring him home again.

After a whole series of appetising courses I think we actually attacked the goose around 3 o'clock, and did not finish our meal until somewhere around 4.30: and I never know what happened to the patients on that afternoon.

He was a very impressive figure in his Church, and when he took a wedding service he appeared to be ten feet tall. There was no question of mumbling through the service, every single word was given its full value: and when he came to 'Those whom God hath joined together, let no man put asunder', my wife and I had a feeling that it would take a lot to get that couple unstuck.

In her lifetime the outstanding personality of the neighbourhood was Lady Warwick. I knew her for about seven years, and looked after her during that time. She was extraordinarily kind to me, although she must have been at least half a century older. I first met her after a meeting in what used to be the old Town Hall, now the local estate agent's offices. It was dark when we came out, and she was having trouble with her motor car: I did not know who she was but asked if I could help her and she told me it was a new car that day and she could not find the lights or the self-starter. I remember that it was a B.S.A. with the new pre-selector gears; luckily I did know how they worked, and was able to help her. She asked me my name, and I told her

32

that I had recently taken over Dr Tench's practice.

Some months later I was summoned to Easton Lodge. The main house was shut up at the time, and she was living in the library wing. There seemed to be hundreds of dogs; she was taking them in, when otherwise they would have been destroyed by the R.S.P.C.A.: most of them were ill and the large room was in considerable confusion. I noticed that the dish out of which they were feeding was the most magnificent great famille rose dish.

After I had finished my consultation, the butler showed me out, gave me an envelope with her ladyship's compliments, saying at the same time that she apologised that it was not in gold.

During the next few years I saw a little of her at intervals. There was a wonderful party she gave for her granddaughter when we received invitations for an At Home 3.0 p.m. to 1.30 a.m., 'Tea, dancing, bridge, concert: dress as you please.' All the neighbourhood was there, and we left at about six o'clock to go home and change for the evening. We sat down, I don't know how many of us, to a magnificent supper, and there was a band and dancing. Bars were scattered about inside the house and through the gardens, but it was a party which was talked about for many years to come.

Her granddaughter has given me her own account of this coming-out party (August 1936):

'The invitation read: "A Merrie Party 3.0 onwards" etc. The guests consisted of local County Council officials, church dignitaries, including several bishops with their families. A spectacular entrance by the Mayor of Southend, wearing his chain of office. I was told by my aunt Queenie Beckett (somewhat hysterically) that the Mayor of Southend had been invited because Granny had met him the previous spring in a remedial mud bath in Southend (rheumatism troubled Lady Warwick in later life). There was only one band, that of the Grenadier Guards, which was laid on by cousin Guy Rasch who was then Colonel-in-Chief. This band played on the lawn all afternoon (rousing marches), in the evening it moved to the Italian Garden and played dance music. Dancing on York stones round the lily pond was slippery because it had rained all morning. Inside the house the "Old Tyme Singers" entertained in Victorian dress — folk songs, Strauss waltzes and so on. Basil Dean loaned coloured floodlights from Ealing film studios, as well as the electricians to operate them: this gave a beautiful effect to the garden after dark — but what did those electricians think when they moved their lights over so many bishops, mayors, etc! There were no young people and I was given no invitations to send out, but was allowed one "best friend" to stay and could not have done without her. My mother was very troubled because I was so "bolshey" about the party all the weeks beforehand. The "best friend" never left my side and I suspect she was bribed to make sure I did not try to escape!'

When this same granddaughter was ill as quite a young girl, I once went up to see her and as I walked through the large mahogany door into the big Edwardian bedroom, a plate shattered on the wall over my head. The girl disappeared under the bedclothes, and the irate elderly nanny pulled them back whereupon she exclaimed, 'So sorry, doctor, I thought it was only nanny.'

In due course Lady Warwick became ill, and there was no doubt that this was a final illness. I suggested an opinion in London, and she went up in state to stay at the Connaught Hotel where Lord Dawson and Mr Dickson-Wright were due to see her in the afternoon. Beforehand Lady Warwick presented me with a cheque book saying that she had signed a couple of blank cheques and would I please deal with that side of the business. It rather gave me pleasure to find myself as paymaster to these eminent gentlemen, especially as Dickson-Wright had been my chief at St Mary's only a few years previously. As nothing could be done, she came home to live the rest of her time quietly, but towards the end she became uncomfortable and I suggested that she should see Lord Dawson again, but she said, 'Oh, I couldn't trouble poor Bertie to come down here, and I am certainly not fit enough to go up and see him. So I tell you what, doctor, you go up and tell him about me.' So I did this, and had tea with him while he regaled me with racy medical anecdotes of all the Edwardian society of the pre first world war era. The sad thing is that the stories came so thick and fast that I was quite unable to remember any of them by the time he said goodbye to me on the front doorstep: when it suddenly occurred to me that we had not in fact discussed Lady Warwick at all. I said I must have one word about her, whereupon he replied, 'I know. She will be complain-

34

ing of constipation. She'll want something to help her there. I would suggest bile beans.' So I went home and Lady Warwick said to me eagerly, 'Well, what did he say?' and I replied that he had thought about her carefully, and decided the answer to her problems would be 'bile beans'. Lady Warwick sighed contentedly and said, 'Ah, I knew he would be able to help me. Bile Beans. Yes, that shall be it.' Two or three weeks later she died peacefully, and even at that great age she had a youthful beauty and freshness which I do not remember seeing elsewhere.

One might go straight from Easton Lodge to a gypsy caravan and again to a striking character, for this was one of the regular gypsy neighbourhoods, and some families would return year after year for the various crops which needed extra casual labour such as hoeing sugarbeet and later lifting it, pea picking, potato gathering, and so on. They usually went to the same encampment and some of the green lanes were never without a number of caravans dotted about: they were the old horse caravans, and plenty of horses, dogs and children. It was part of their way of life to look after their own illnesses; birth was regarded as a normal affair; and the doctor was usually only called in when there was a death: but when I came here they were beginning to use the district nurse regularly and she would call in one of the doctors if she got into difficulties; and the doctor was consulted for accidents and for more serious illness in a way which past generations had avoided. I always got on well with them, and made some good friends. Apart from a very few exceptions, they were grateful, uncomplaining; they always paid cash, and I found them very genuine good patients.

I had been out visiting all day, and came in to find a gypsy sitting in the waiting room with his ten year old son. The maid told me that they had come just after I had left the morning surgery, and when she said I was not going to be in until tea-time they just said, 'We can wait', and sat patiently. I asked what was the matter and the father said that the boy had been splitting logs and that a chip had flown up and embedded in his eye. I lifted the swollen lid, and there was the end of the splinter sticking up, having gone between the eye and the bone of the eye socket but the eye itself had escaped damage. It looked a fairly hefty

35

chunk of wood, and I asked the father how big he thought it was to which he replied an inch or two long. The nearest casualty department was Chelmsford Hospital thirteen miles away, and country doctors tended to do this type of thing themselves: I offered to give the boy a whiff of ethyl chloride but his father said no, he'd bear the pain so I got a firm grip on the end of the splinter with a pair of forceps and pulled gently and then more strongly until I felt that I must pull the entire eye out! With my fingers against the eye I finally pulled out a great chunk of wood an inch and a half long and tapering down from a quarter of an inch to a fine point.

On another occasion I was called by the district nurse at High Easter seven miles away, to a woman who had had a large number of children, she thought eight or nine, and who had developed eclampsia, a condition which was extremely dangerous in those days both to the mother and her unborn baby, a fortnight before her next baby was due. I told the husband that she needed immediate treatment in hospital, but his wife absolutely refused to go, and he himself was equally definite that nothing would induce them to allow her to go in. I pointed out the danger to her life and in any case the distance from a doctor. Whereupon he dived under the mattress in the caravan and produced a large roll of very dirty one pound notes — it was three to four inches across and tightly bound with string and said:

'See here doctor, I've saved all this money. You can have the lot if you'll let me harness up my horse and bring the caravan into your yard in Dunmow. You can look after her there and we needn't go to hospital.'

I told him his wife's life was worth more than any money, and he suddenly gave in and he drove his wife in the caravan into the hospital. Three weeks later they came together into the surgery at High Easter with the new arrival to thank me and to present me with a couple of the notes from his bundle.

I had seen a gypsy woman in a caravan one day with the nurse because of some difficulty in her confinement. It was winter, and I had other visits to pay further on, so I came back a couple of hours later just to check that all was well. Dusk had fallen on a real wintry evening, with snow flurries already beginning to lie in the frozen furrows. The usual clamour of barking and cries of children greeted my torch as

I made my way to my patient's caravan, and I noticed as I went up the steps that there was a soap box with a bundle inside it on the shelf beside the door. The mother was all right, and I asked after the baby — 'Oh, she's outside' — and there she was, nice and pink, but her only covering was a dirty threadbare blanket. I asked if this was usual for a new-born baby, and the man replied, 'Well, doctor, you know we're poor: it's another girl and we've plenty of them already. We can't afford to keep weak ones, so we'll just see in the morning.'

It is the custom when the old people die to burn the caravan. I believe that it must apply to the last survivor of the pair, for in the only case where I knew of it the husband had died first, and the old lady lived on in the caravan for a couple of years before she died. In fact she probably was the owner of the caravan, as she had always been a proper matriarch and it had seemed to me that it was her word which was law rather than that of her husband. She was an old friend whom I had seen a great deal of, I used to be received with great courtesy and there could never be any question of a hurried visit as there was a ritual of enquiry on her part about my family and on my part about hers. Her face was almost black and deeply creased all over but in her youth she must have been a rare beauty: her hands were very small and fine, and both she herself and the inside of her caravan were scrupulously clean. With the burning of her caravan, her families abandoned the camp and moved into council houses: one of the small children went to school and learned to read and write, so that she always accompanied any member of the family who had to come to the doctor and was explained, 'Our Phoebe is the scholar, so she'll do any of the book work for us.'

Some of the postmen were great characters. One couple I remember well: their home was a small cottage on the Downs in Dunmow which is always a blaze of flowers. He had retired, and was himself the son of a former postman, and even while he lived his own son and grandson were in the post office as well, making four generations. He died, and the old lady lived on in the cottage and was active and did her garden and went down to church regularly every Sunday evening. She was over eighty when she got pneumonia, and I looked after her at home with the help of a daughter and she did well: but she became very distressed as Sunday evening came round and begged me to allow her to go down to service. She was quite prepared to hire a taxi for it and she was very sad when I told her she must not. She said that she had been to church every Sunday evening for the whole of her life, and especially it was precious to her because that was how she got married. The story was this:

When she left school she went to help as a maid and later barmaid at a public house called The White Lion which has now been pulled down. One evening a handsome young postman came in for his pint, and they chatted and liked the look of each other. As he went out he asked her if she got any time off and whether she would come out with him, and she replied that she had Sunday afternoon and evening off but that she always went to church. He pulled a face and she said, 'Look, if I come out with you in the afternoon you shall come to Church with me in the evening' and so it was a bargain, and in due course they went to the same church to get married, and she had been every Sunday evening since. However, I assured her that I would see the vicar and would ask him to bring Communion up to her during the following week and she was content.

CHAPTER III

THE DOCTOR AT WORK

In Dr Tench's house the surgery opened into a passage which gave into a small room, combining waiting room and dispensary. A bench ran along the wall under the window and patients were called up from this in turn to a screen of wood and frosted glass behind which were the doctor's desk and rows of shelves crammed with bottles and a counter. This was where he consulted. He knew all his patients well, and there was a subdued series of questions and answers about the present complaint, with the row of waiting patients all only a few feet away, straining their ears to hear any snippy bits. Sometimes a blouse would be loosened behind the screen, or a shirt button undone, and the chest piece of his stethoscope would be slid inside, or down the back. Then the advice would be given or a bottle of medicine concocted. On rare occasions Dr Tench would take his patient through to the cluttered up back consulting room for some more intimate examination, but there was no running water, only an old upright washstand made of iron for which a maid had to be summoned to supply water. For an abdominal or vaginal examination he would send the patient home to bed and call later.

To return to the dispensary, next to the desk was a sink, emptying into a large bucket. Over the sink there was a cider barrel suspended in the ceiling with a tube running down to a clip out of which water could be drawn to fill the bottles. A maid used to come down the long passage from the house to fill up this cask every morning, bringing with her a pair of steps and a tall brass jug of water: if during a surgery the water began to run a tinge of green, I knew that it was getting low and I went in search of a maid to refill it. When Dr Tench was ill I used to go and see him after the evening surgery, and he would eagerly enquire, 'How many barrels today, my boy?' If I said two he would say it was good, if I said three, he would comment, 'You're going down well.' The passage from the surgery door led on past the dispensary to the rarely used consulting room. Chief amongst the main pieces of furniture was the old upright piano already mentioned. Another piece of furniture was a

Victorian horsehair couch which was also covered with unopened parcels, journals and so on. There was a desk in whose drawers I was told were the records of the patients, but all I found was a jumble of x-ray films and letters from consultants in no sort of order at all. In fact all the records he kept were in his day book and his ledger, and there was a complicated method of identifying the medicine by the number of the page in the ledger from when it was dispensed. If I looked this up, I would as likely as not find it was simply a repeat of a previous page which again had to be traced right back to the beginning.

All medicines were mixed up from the individual constituents; each bottle needed four or five different extracts and tinctures, so this took time, but the mystique of dispensing was obviously part of the treatment of the patient, who would watch with awe at the various ingredients being carefully selected and measured! This was just as well, for the majority of drugs had little if any pharmacological effect, although there is no doubt that nowadays we realise that a number of them were in fact poisonous (preparations of arsenic and mercury) but usually in such dilutions as to be unlikely to have much serious effect.

Many of these mixtures were made up to the full dose with an 'infusion', which was a watery extract of some flavouring which might have a mild pharmacological effect. The favourite one was an infusion of gentian, but there were others such as infusion of quassia which was used for enemas for threadworms, of rhubarb, and even of digitalis and of ergot. One of the cook's jobs was to prepare these infusions which she did in an earthenware vessel which resembled a huge coffee pot with a strainer in the lip; the raw material was put into this, and boiling water was poured on, and it then simmered on the old black kitchen range for a specified length of time before being allowed to cool and then poured off into another great earthenware jar to cool and mature. When I first married, my wife began this operation as a good young doctor's wife should, but we soon decided that it was simpler to buy the finished product in Winchester jars from the wholesale delivery van of drugs, which came fortnightly.

Leeches were quite a popular form of treatment and I inherited a bowl with half a dozen of these creatures in it along with some weed to keep them happy. Before we were married I was showing my wife over the house and surgery, and I pointed them out to her and remarked 'There ought to be six in there, but I can only see five.' When I looked round there was no sign of her, and she tended to avoid the dispensary on subsequent visits. Mustard plasters were used quite a lot, along with chili paste which used to be rubbed well into the small of the back in cases of lumbago. It certainly gave the patient something else to think about, and the warm glow probably did some good. There was a large bottle which I was told should only be used for the more expensive private patients, it was labelled 'VINUM FERRI': it looked a horrid mess, and I was told on no account to shake it or the sediment would rise in the bottle and spoil it. It turned out that this was concocted by putting a pound of nails into a Winchester jar, and filling it up with cooking sherry. This mixture had to be shaken every day for the next three or four weeks, and then allowed to settle before being bottled. 'Wine of iron' certainly tasted extremely nasty, but anaemic patients appeared to have every confidence in it. All medicines for private patients had to be wrapped individually in special white paper and sealed with sealing wax at each end. The doctor never had a dispenser; he did all this himself. The same wrapping had to be done where the medicine was to be delivered by the local carrier or by the postman.

Tradition played a large part in the effect of medicines. Because rheumatism was so widespread, there was a variety of 'cures' and bee stings were one of the most popular, even to the extent of being exploited commercially. For a time I used a preparation of 'bee venom' of which a small amount of paste was ground into the skin with a strip of fine sandpaper.

Life was dull in the isolated villages so the circle of gossips invented a splendid game of 'medicine tasting'. Each one would come to the house where the doctor called regularly two days a week, and complain of something different, cough, cold, stomach, headache; and when the medicines arrived they would sit down comfortably and pass them round. I got suspicious when they all asked for a drop of 'what did old Mrs Smith's tissick such good.'

One of my neighbouring doctors told me of a horrifying experience that he had once had when he was called out to a child who was choking badly. She suffered from whooping cough, and the parents appeared more frightened than he expected. He opened the child's mouth with some difficulty, and looked down its throat for obstruction: there was obviously something, looking rather like the tail of a mouse. He managed to pull it out with some difficulty, and sure enough it was the best part of a small mouse which had been forcibly given to the child to cure the whooping cough.

Quite an expensive item in setting up in practice is the purchase of a minimum of surgical instruments. The old doctor told me I was welcome to buy any of his that I wanted on a valuation by the local chemist, and this seemed to be a good offer. He had a large quantity, mostly in very bad condition: it was evident that during his career he had done some fairly major operations, and there were a good many which I did not feel I should ever use. In addition there were some museum pieces which I kept and when I used to teach students I would offer half-a-crown to anyone who could tell me what they were.

The prize was a 'tooth-key' which looked like a corkscrew with a series of wicked little toothed blades curved in such a way that they gripped the crown of the tooth and then a twist wrenched the whole thing off sideways. There was a probang, an equally barbarous instrument for extracting foreign bodies that had been swallowed by mistake. It looked like a catheter about a foot long, with a little sponge on the end which was dipped in vaseline: next came a couple of inches of horsehair and then the gum elastic length of catheter with a handle at the top which pulled in and out. The idea was to push this down the gullet beyond the foreign body, and then by pulling the handle the horsehair unfurled itself like a stiff umbrella, and by pulling this back up the gullet anything that was caught there would come up. I suspect that in the majority of cases it was the lining of the gullet itself. Then there was an impressive instrument called a plessor and pleximeter, a gong stick with which you tapped on a highly polished round ebony chest piece. It was simply a more impressive way of percussing a chest or abdomen. For measuring a chest and the relative flattening in early tuberculous infection, there was a pair of long flexible lead rods hinged together so that they could be folded and pressed against the body and then opened on the hinge and closed again on a sheet of paper:

so that one could draw an accurate transverse section of the chest at any point. Finally there was an apparatus for bleeding and cupping. The cupping instrument was a little square brass box with half a dozen slots in which very sharp knives rotated on a spring. You wound it up, turned a screw to adjust the depth to which you wanted it to cut, put it on the skin and pressed the trigger — the result was half a dozen nice little vertical slices over which you then put a glass cup with a large rubber ball.

One of the advantages of an isolated country practice is variety, out-of-hours dentistry for instance, for villages and small towns tended to depend on the chemists and on the doctor for having teeth pulled out: proper dentists were few annd far between in the country, and tended to be regarded by farm workers as something 'for the gentry only'. Dr Tench had a complete set of dental forceps which he passed on to me, and which I used for some years when the visiting dentist was not in Dunmow. He only came one day a week, and by the time a patient asked to have a tooth out it usually involved an abscess which needed draining quickly. The local chemist was extremely adept at doing it, and I took it as a compliment when people came to me in preference to him.

Once a week the local doctors used to give gas for their patients who were having extractions at the dentist's, and we usually had to do half a dozen in the half hour which meant a fairly quick turn over, and hygiene was completely lacking. The gas machine consisted of two cylinders bolted together on the floor, and the release valve was operated by one's foot to fill the bag. The face piece was all in one and the technique was to get the patient sufficiently far out so that all the necessary teeth could be extracted before he or she came round. This needed fairly precise judgment which only came with practice, and it meant that the dentist had to work as fast as he could. One with whom I worked longest was a really expert extractor indeed: he fairly whipped the teeth out, and he threw them wildly over his shoulder and made no attempt to do more than kick them under his bookcase before the next patient came in. I remember the look of absolute horror as a rather fastidious lady came in to have a tooth out and skidded on a bunch of recently extracted teeth which he had not had time to clear up.

A friend of mine told me of how he had gone out to give

an anaesthetic to a farmer's wife. It was a total extraction, and he had to use chloroform to get her sufficiently anaesthetised, but it was all quite straightforward and the dentist whipped out the entire range of teeth.

While she was coming round the dentist walked about the room collecting the teeth that he'd thrown in all directions, and he took the bowl to the window and called to the doctor, 'Like to see something?' Hens were pecking round the farmyard below, the dentist made a clucking noise and threw the teeth out to them, when there was a wild scramble and within five seconds not a tooth was to be seen!

A doctor is expected to get all sorts of odd things out of any of the openings of the body, mostly the nostrils and ears of small children. Each one presents a problem to one's ingenuity which can be rather fun. One small child was brought to me at an out-surgery with a lead soldier up her nose: the mother was an intelligent woman, and had brought me ditto from the same set, from which I saw that the soldier was holding a fixed bayonet out at a right angle, and it was this which had got into the mucous membrane of the nose.

I put the child out with a whiff of ethyl chloride on a handkerchief and then I was able to snip through the bayonet where it joined the main body of the soldier, when the whole thing tumbled out quite easily.

A cowrie shell in a child's ear at the seaside, and a sunflower seed in a nostril are two others I can remember.

A young farmer came to see me and asked to have his ears syringed as he was getting married the following week. I had some difficulty on one side, because underneath the superficial wax there was a green object. It tookme quite a long time to get out a fairly large seedling, and I showed it to him in the bowl whereupon he roared with laughter. I asked him what was so funny and he said, 'Well, doctor, you know about my marriage, it's a shotgun affair. We're fond of each other but I'm having to get married in a hurry: you know what that seedling is? It's a wild oat.'

The doctor was paid in various ways, by private patients, by the national health insurance ('The Lloyd George'), by provident dispensaries of various sorts, and finally as the parish doctor by the local authority. It was quite a job sorting into which category the patient should fit, and fees were always months or even years behind-hand: in fact I was told when I started in general practice that I would have to go for my first years with very little to live on. This sounded bad, but as all the tradespeople worked on the same principle, and it was literally two years before I could get an account out of the local chemist, it was not so serious as it sounded. Old Dr Tench only used to send in his accounts once a year, but he advised me to shorten the period to six months: in fact I started sending them out every quarter and patients were quite sympathetic, understanding that as a young doctor starting I did need the money rather sooner than they were accustomed to paying the old doctor. Fees varied in the case of private patients, according to what the doctor thought they could afford, and they ranged from 3/6d. for a visit and medicine, up to one guinea. A consultation in the surgery cost half-a-crown to the poorest private patient, and that included one bottle of medicine (without which the consultation was never considered to be complete) and I do not think that even the wealthiest patients ever paid more than 7/6d. if they came to see the doctor. Again, Dr Tench advised me to look at this question and to adjust my fees to more modern standards: I was taught a useful lesson quite early on by one patient who was an extremely wealthy stockbroker. This man had a one-eyed horse, and it was his habit to ride up to the pub every morning and return at lunch time, leaving the horse to find its way back without much help from him. One day he fell off and broke two ribs, and I went out and strapped him up and looked after him carefully, visiting him every day for about three weeks. At my last visit he said, 'Doctor, you're young, and have just started, so I expect you would like me to pay your bill straight away': so I sent him an account for two guineas. He asked me to go and see him about it, and said: 'I don't want to have to change my doctor, but if you ever insult me by sending in such a paltry bill again, then I shall have to!' I looked after him until he died, and had many a day's hunting in his old pair of Maxwell hunting boots.

It was rare for patients not to pay their bills eventually, and when I compared my percentage of bad debts with those of my contemporaries I was amazed at the honesty of the country folk, who on the whole had lower incomes than almost everybody else.

The next category of patient was the old national health

insurance that used to be known as 'The Lloyd George'. These were only wage earners and there was a capitation fee of 10/- per head to the doctor with a very small additional annual fee if you provided medicine, I think it was a matter of about 6/-, and also a small mileage fee. Shortly after I went into practice in the depression of 1930/31, we had to take a cut of ten per cent in all government salaries, so that the capitation fee came down to 9/-: and this was not restored for several years. I had about 600 patients on this list, and all the records were kept in a cardboard box underneath the sofa in the dining room. At intervals of about a year an inspector used to come round from the Ministry to see that these records were being properly kept, and also to inspect the poisons register and to see that the poisons were kept locked up. It was very decent of him to give several days notice, but obviously the ministry officials realised that this was necessary for country doctors: the cardboard box used to be pulled out and dusted, and at meal times Mrs Tench would read out the names of the patients so that the old doctor could tell her between mouthfuls what numbers to put down in the appropriate columns for consultations, visits or certificates; with a brief diagnosis in the notes section. He told me that he was usually complimented for keeping his records at all.

The agricultural wage was 28/-, and on that it was quite obvious that a man could not pay private fees to a doctor for looking after his family. So for many years 'provident associations' such as the Buffaloes, the Oddfellows, and the Dunmow association had been founded to organise a weekly or monthly payment from their members out of which they could pay both sickness benefit and a capitation fee to the doctor. In fact these were the very rudimentary forerunners of the mechanism of the present National Health Service. Incidentally the hospital side was covered by the Hospital Saving Association, and the district nurses in the same way had their associations with contributions covering the nursing at home. Contributions were in the nature of only a few pennies per week, and a large number of the farm workers belonged to one or other of these 'Clubs'.

The doctor also had his own little 'dispensary' for patients who did not belong to any other organisation but who were not so destitute that they had to go 'on the parish'. Dr

Tench's particular dispensary asked for a quarterly payment of 2/6d. for which he gave both treatment and medicine, but confinements and broken limbs were extra: children were 1/6d.: and at the beginning of each quarter a lot of time was spent in marking off these small contributions.

Finally for the extremely poor there was the parish doctor. An important man in the community was the 'Relieving Officer' who was the clerk to the parish guardians and who decided whether a person qualified for parish relief. This could take the form of vouchers for coal or clothing or individual items such as a bed: and also entitlement to the parish doctor. Each of us were allotted to certain parishes, and when I came I found that old Dr Tench looked after half a dozen parishes in the neighbourhood and Dr Hall and his partner looked after the other half. It meant that if a patient moved house he or she might have to change their doctor, and it also meant that two different doctors would often have to visit the same house if husband and wife were both down with illness, one being on the national health list of one doctor and the other being in the parish of another. Dr Hall and I agreed that this was absolute nonsense, but it took us several years before we could persuade the parish guardians to pool our salaries and our fields of work, so that we were paid half each and the parish patients could have a choice of doctor.

The wage of 28/- was expected to cover a working man and his wife and four children: after that he could apply for an extra 5/- a week for any child over the four, so that a new baby which could be breast fed for a year meant a considerable addition to his income. At the end of a year the child began to eat and generally to cost as much as the allowance, so mum was encouraged to supplement the income by producing a fresh source of the bonus 5/-. One thin little woman was about to have her sixth child, and I told her it would be dangerous to have any more whereupon she replied:

'But, doctor, I can suckle them up to a year, and the extra 5/- comes in very handy to feed the rest.'

I think that this certainly did account for some of the very large families that I found amongst the poorest farmworkers, and which of course led to considerable prosperity when they all became adult wage-earners, particularly as wages improved. There was one house I remember as very

47

poor when I first arrived, with seven or eight children, but a dozen years later during the war I noticed that the general standard of living was as high as any of the farmhouses, with motor bicycles and even one or two cars parked outside.

CHAPTER IV

DISEASES AND CASES

It was the custom for a new doctor to call on all neighbouring doctors. Nearly all of them were very friendly and
encouraging but they varied in their advice to me: one very
sardonic looking gentleman said, 'I suppose quite a few of
my patients will leave me and come to you, but don't get
above yourself, my boy, because they're only the riff raff.
They changed to me when I first came, and they'll change
again: half of them never paid me as they didn't the chap
they changed from! Anyway, always give a gloomy
prognosis, you'll find it pays. If you're wrong, they're only
too pleased: whereas if you're right they think what a clever
chap you are.' But another doctor gave me exactly the
opposite advice. He said, 'However grave you think the
case is, and you know you can do absolutely nothing, there
is one thing you can do: always leave them hope.'

I think the most valuable piece of advice that I was given
was from Dr Allman Hall who was my 'opponent' in
Dunmow, and my very good friend. I gathered that my
predecessor was not always on very good terms with his
neighbours, but this seemed nonsense to me for Dr Hall
could not have been kinder to a newcomer. He said, 'When
you get called out at night, however much you feel like
cursing, go first and curse afterwards, because you'll find
you never do.' I found this was so true, because however
bad a temper I was in when I arrived, I found eager faces,
smiles of relief that someone now had come to take charge
of the situation, lights on in the neighbouring houses; a
general murmur of relief and a feeling that now it would be
all right. Frequently all that the doctor did in fact was to
quieten a mass hysteria.

Apart from the doctors, there was a good deal of calling
by people in the neighbourhood who came to see what the
new doctor and his wife were like. Many of them were
patients of the old doctor who wanted to judge for
themselves whether they should continue with that practice:
and we had to become accustomed to finding a good deal of
pleasant small talk around teatime. Once when we had been
out together on a muddy walk in the country, we got back

to the maid who said, 'There's a lot of them called this afternoon, and I didn't think you'd be long, so I've told them to wait.' We were using one of the smaller rooms as a sitting room, while the drawing room was slowly being furnished, and when we went in there was standing room only for some of the callers. I had a little smooth haired fox terrier puppy who followed me in: but when he saw all these strangers he yelped his disapproval and dived for cover, which was underneath the enormous black skirts of the extremely disagreeable wife of one of the local parsons. Nothing would induce him to come out beyond an occasional furtive peep, and it certainly broke the ice for everybody else in the room, but the old lady never forgave me.

Saturday night used to be a big night in the surgery until I stopped it after about five years. I only had the courage to do so because the other doctors did the same; in fact we used to set examples to each other in slowly throwing off the complete tyranny of the patient. When I first came patients rang the surgery bell and did not ask if the doctor could see them but simply if he was in, taking it as completely axiomatic that if he were in he would attend them, and the doctor's widow used to say to me during my first days here, 'If you want to get peace from the patients you have got to get right out and away and off the telephone!' But in my first years there was always a lot of work on a Saturday evening, partly because people felt they could not go over the Sunday for they did not like to disturb the doctor on that day, and also because things happened on Saturday afternoon. An occasional but by no means rare occurrence was when beaters got peppered with shot. I had been at a shoot with R. A. Butler, then MP for Saffron Walden, and had a very beautiful shoot over the Broxted and Tilty area, and one of the guns had definitely peppered a beater. I told him to come in for me to take the pellets out of his face, and sure enough after tea I was busy taking them out and putting them into a kidney dish. As I turned away to wash my hands I heard a faint clink behind me. There was a mirror above the wash basin and in it I saw the man dropping pellets into the dish out of his pocket. I said, 'How much do you get per pellet?' and he said, 'Oh, the standard rate is £1 a pellet.' I looked in the kidney dish where I had put seven pellets, picked out five more and threw them away, putting the genuine ones into an envelope which I then signed as containing seven which had been taken out by me, and I thought he'd done quite well for the evening's work!

Another Saturday night there was a good deal of hub-bub outside the surgery door and the maid who answered the bell (and we had two maids even until after the war) announced that they'd brought in a man from Newton Green who was in a very bad way. I found an old friend who had got very drunk indeed: he had succeeded in getting upstairs but at the top he had lost his balance and had fallen backwards the whole length, breaking his wrist and cutting his bald scalp clean across so that the flap hung down in a rakish way over his eyes. The odd thing was that it was bleeding very little. The ambulance service was erratic, and even less likely to function on a Saturday evening, so that casualties were always brought straight to the doctor and he was expected to patch them up and keep them until they could be moved to hospital by whatever transport could be magicked up. In fact the man presented very little difficulty, for his alcohol acted as a perfectly satisfactory analgesic if not anaesthetic. He talked away in a confused and blurred tone while I reduced his fracture and put it on a splint, and then set about repairing his head. For years afterwards he always shook hands whenever he met me and took off his hat to show me what a beautiful scar I had left him with.

I was told that one of the greatest attractions to maids working in the doctor's house was the excitement of the surgery door, the real blood to be scrubbed off the doorstep each morning.

In those days of single-handed practice an anaesthetic was a problem. Ordinarily one would try to get one of the other doctors to come round, but on Saturday night we were all pretty busy; so that my wife was liable to be pressed into service, and she was not then so occupied with cooking the dinner as we had a full-time cook to do that. The anaesthetic used to be 'a la reine' given from a drop bottle of chloroform and ether in equal parts on to an open mask. After induction which I did myself, I handed over a bottle of pure ether to my wife and she gave further drops as I told her: keeping an eye on the patient at the same time as I was either reducing a fracture or incising the abscess (in those days before antibiotics, draining of pus was the most important thing a doctor could do to prevent the spread of infection). In time my wife became quite an expert.

There was a woman patient of about forty, with one small son of six. Two years before, her heart had begun to beat irregularly, and she finally developed paroxysmal tachycardia: it caused her considerable distress and discomfort with breathlessness and palpitation. She became quite seriously ill. She was able to do her usual household work between attacks, but I did think that it would be wise for her to be seen by a heart specialist.

There were no specialists as such in this neighbourhood at all in those days, the hospitals were staffed by general practitioners, each of whom specialised in a particular subject: but no physician at the local hospital thirteen miles away could really be called a heart specialist and there was no electrocardiograph nearer, than London. My old chief came down on a sunny summer afternoon and we saw the patient together. He gave a good prognosis, and was rewarded by his fee of a guinea a mile plus five guineas for the consultation which came to just under fifty pounds. It was produced in fairly grubby notes from the till of the shop run by the husband.

The doctor then came back to tea with myself and my wife in the garden at the pleasant old Georgian house in the high street. Cucumber sandwiches and China tea out in the garden, and off he went in his Rolls Royce back to London: but he had hardly gone when the maid came out to me to say that the patient's husband was at the surgery door asking to see me urgently. He told me that his wife had just died suddenly.

Appointment systems in general have only recently come in, and over thirty years ago the door was opened twice a day to the waiting room, and patients trooped in to wait and be seen in order. They sat on a bench round the room and gossiped until each one was called in separately, and it was all a very friendly affair.

In the middle of an evening surgery the wife of one of the local publicans came in complaining with her chest. She had been breathless and uncomfortable, and I asked her to take off her things down to her waist and get up on the couch. The patient was a very big heavy woman, who had smoked a great deal in her time and had a smoker's cough and a husky voice. She climbed on to the couch with difficulty, and I examined the front of her chest as well as I could. Then I asked her to lean forwards so that I could get at her back, but she started to cough when she changed her position. I gave her a little time and then asked her to try again but the same thing happened, and I suppose I got a little bit irritated and said that she really could stop coughing if she tried hard, so she did and I got on with listening to the back of her chest. To my surprise I heard nothing at all. Her weight became more heavy against my stethoscope and she finally fell back and I realised that she was dead.

I could hear my dispenser through the little hatch into the dispensary and waiting room: she was laughing and joking with the row of patients on the benches. I opened the hatch and asked her to come through, and I think she must have realised that there was something amiss for there was a sudden hush in the waiting room as she walked past the benches and they saw what must have been a set and anxious face. She was a young girl, and had not seen a dead body before, but she behaved splendidly and went out to tell the patients that they would have to go away as the one I was examining had become seriously ill.

In those days it was usual for isolated country doctors to do their own post mortems, but I do not remember doing this one and I think I may have persuaded the pathologist at a local hospital to do it for me as I was so closely involved. There was a massive coronary thrombosis.

I suppose the most prevalent diseases were bronchitis and rheumatism; the 'rheumatics' was accepted by a farm labourer as the result of endless insults to his joints through carrying heavy loads over rough ground in any sort of weather, and often not being completely dry for weeks on end. Infectious diseases in those days were killers, there was no organised immunisation yet against diphtheria, and scarlet fever was a dreaded disease with its consequent mastoids, nephritis and valvular heart disease. Often the family contacts of the case with the rash would develop the fever and complications, for doctors did not then realise that it was the infection by the streptococcus which caused the illness, and that the rash only occurred in some of the infected patients. We had a little local isolation hospital in Dunmow, which was looked after by one of the local G.P.s, with advice if he wanted it from the Medical Officer of

Health in Braintree. Tuberculosis was common, the pulmonary type nearly always ended in a lingering death: the bovine type caused the septic neck glands and joint diseases which resulted in hunchback (Potts disease) and in stiff knees and hips.

Osteomyelitis (bone abscess) was only too frequent in children and the eventual outcome of the disease depended on rapid operation: this in turn was followed by a long and most painful period of drainage and dressings so that the child took a very long time to recover, and often was left with a permanent disability. Rheumatic fever with heart disease turned healthy children into permanent semi-invalids; there was not much venereal disease, at any rate recognised at that time, but I had a number of the late effects of untreated disease both in men and women. There was a certain amount of rickets; its most serious form was in women who had suffered from it in childhood, and whose pelvis had been softened and narrowed by the pressure of their hip joints so as to produce a 'clover leaf effect'. The old doctor did not do any antenatal examination, and I was looked on with considerable suspicion when I insisted on examining these young women before their babies were due, 'it was not quite right for the young doctor to want to see so much of them'. We had been taught to use a larger caliper called a 'pelvimeter' and to depend on various external measurements with this, but it only gave a rough guide, and in any case did not show the critical internal narrowing which could only be shown by x-rays, or found out when labour was delayed. Internal examination would reveal the severe cases only.

How did the doctor cope with these illnesses? He usually worked on his own, sometimes in a partnership of two, and the surgery was always part of the private house. Only a few of the drugs which were used then have survived the last forty years; morphine, atropine and digitalis are among the most important survivors, along with various forms of antacid such as simple bicarbonate of soda, bismuth carbonate and aluminium hydroxide. And the basic expectorant cough medicines have not altered very much, although heroin is now frowned upon: it was most effective in those days and I do not remember anyone becoming addicted although it may be that I was not on the look out!

A great deal more attention was paid to the details of

nursing, partly because of the lay ignorance of the ordinary principles, and partly because of the poverty of the homes and lack of bare essentials. In fact nursing was about all one could do in a good deal of serious respiratory diseases including pneumonia and pulmonary tuberculosis: and the infectious diseases appeared both to be more severe and to be liable to complications which consisted of secondary infection against which there were no antibiotics. Steam kettles were used in respiratory distress, and in diphtheria: in pneumonia there was great attention paid to the 'crisis' which is never seen nowadays but was most dramatic. The infection of the lungs would spread rapidly for five or six days, with a profound constitutional disturbance, high fever, sweating, delirium and constant hard cough: this reached a climax and the patient would either lapse into a coma and die, or would fall into a deep sleep from which he would wake, and although very weak he would appear to be his normal self and with a normal temperature and pulse, quite keen to take food, to sleep, and to gain strength rapidly. In the stages up to the crisis the doctor might use morphine to control the cough, digitalis to help a failing heart, and especially judicious doses of alcohol (usually in the form of brandy), which in fact was used for a great many conditions, and was very effective both as a stimulus for a failing heart, and as a sedative at night for elderly people who were accustomed to it, the traditional 'night cap'; and in typhoid and acute diarrhoea.

Country doctors were expected to do their own casualty work. Farming folk would have been astonished to be told to travel a dozen miles to the hospital and in any case there was only very sparse public transport so that a good deal of minor surgery was done in the consulting room, especially the draining of abscesses where accurate judgment and experience were needed to determine the precise moment when pus had formed and should be let out. The management of the acute ear was completely different from nowadays, as many doctors including myself held that it was essential to incise the drum as soon as pain, bulging and pyrexia had occurred. The object was to prevent the collection of pus which could track back into the mastoid, and this treatment certainly did seem to result in fewer 'glue ears' than we see today when they have been treated with antibiotics.

Fractures were very often treated by the family doctor and splinted after setting (only sometimes under an anaesthetic) and as an x-ray involved a visit to hospital 13 miles away a straight-forward Colles fracture and a Potts would usually be set first and x-rayed if necessary afterwards. Wooden splints were used a good deal, although I personally always preferred to make my own plaster ones: and this involved using the loose powder wetted in a bowl and ladled on to the bandage as one wound it on. It was a messy business but sometimes produced very good results.

Wounds were cleaned and stitched up, but where tendons or nerves were involved we tried to send them into the local hospital: but it was quite usual for us to amputate one or two joints of fingers when they had been severely crushed or lacerated and if there was a reasonable amount of undamaged skin to make a satisfactory flap with a scar on the dorsum. This was done under a nerve block and Esbach bandage. Hydrocoeles, ascites and pleural effusions used to be tapped by the G.P. either in his surgery or in the patient's home and for high blood pressure it was usual to venesect a pint of blood using a glass bottle and a vacuum pump. Retention of urine was dealt with by a catheter, and a great many more strictures were seen in those days. Some of these needed dilating once a week even for years on end with gum elastic catheters: and there was invariably urinary infection which was treated with potassium citrate and mandelic acid alternately to keep changing the reaction of the urine.

In addition there were the ritual operations beginning with snipping the tongue-tie in the new born baby, and usually accompanied by the wellworn joke in the case of a girl, 'Her husband won't thank me for doing this, will he?' Small boys were always circumcised if they belonged to the middle or upper classes, and finally at anything from four years old onwards, tonsils and adenoids were 'removed'. As the operation was usually done with an old-fashioned guillotine under a rapid anaesthetic with ethyl chloride, the operation was often repeated at intervals during childhood. At the same time experienced ENT surgeons could make a remarkably effective job of it with these same rather primitive tools, and there is no doubt of the very considerable benefit that the operation did give to some children who were constantly choked right up with huge infected tonsils which never seemed to clear up, and which are not seen so much nowadays because of the effect of antibiotics.

A great deal of attention was paid to quarantine and isolation for infectious diseases, with the result that epidemics were considerably prolonged; for most of the children got it in the end, or, if they did not, they saved it up for later life when they would catch it from their own children, (and be far more ill as adults). Scarlet fever, diphtheria and sometimes severe cases of measles would be transferred to the isolation hospital, and these varied from very good to quite appalling. The one in Dunmow was in St Edmund's Lane, a name which had originated from Dead Man's Lane because that was where the old pest house stood. The hospital was maintained by the local authority, and there was a matron living in the house which also had a garage where the old ambulance lived. She was responsible for taking calls for the ambulance, and sending off (usually her maid on foot or bicycle) to the ambulance driver who who was a part-time mechanic at the local garage nearly a mile away, or at his home which was only half that distance. The ambulance was a relic of the first world war; it had been fitted on to a de Dion Bouton chassis, and sometimes took quite a time to coax into life. It had to be cranked by hand as it had no self-starter. The hospital went for weeks on end without any patients, but when they were admitted other nurses used to be called in, lysol sheets where hung over the doors, and fumigation carried out in an enormous metal drum into which clothing, bedding, books and so on were put before the boiler underneath was lit up, and sometimes sulphur was introduced through the pipes.

In 1930 very little was known about virus diseases, and we had even less effective drugs to help the patients in an acute attack. Every few years a very virulent form of influenza would occur, sometimes in massive epidemics as in 1918, when I was a schoolboy. I was told afterwards that half the school was down with it, and that several boys died. I myself was one of those who lay unconscious for several days, my relatives quite uncertain as to whether I should ever wake up. In fact when I did, I could not understand how it was that I had missed my birthday by nearly a week.

Once an epidemic was well established there was little

difficulty in recognising the cases, but it was the first case which was so dramatic that it made a vivid impression. An attractive young mother, the wife of the local policeman, became very ill one day. She did not fit into anything that was recognisable and by evening I was so alarmed that I asked a consultant to come down from London. He is now an extremely old and eminent man, but in those days he was young and little known. He had told me when I left hospital that he would always be willing to come down and help me, and that the fee was of minor importance and was simply a matter of whether the patient could afford to pay it or not. In this case I told him on the telephone that he would be unlikely to get more than two or three pounds but he cheerfully drove down and arrived about three hours after I had sent for him. By that time the unfortunate young woman had turned a deep bronze colour and had died of exhaustion. During the next week two of her close friends were also dead: they had been at tea with her the evening before she was taken ill.

'Captain of the men of death' was how pulmonary tuberculosis was described when I was a student. From the first time that somebody spat into their handkerchief and saw bloodstains, to the last stages of coughing away their lives, used to span a matter of two to four years, and when I took over in 1930 from Dr Tench, he had half a dozen of these cases scattered around in the neighbourhood. Several were in farmhouses, and I can think of two of these where successive members of the family lay dying over a period of seven or eight years. They were young adults, and as one girl died the sister who nursed her would develop the cough and in due course take the sister's place in the bedroom. It was the father and mother, the elderly couple, who survived: they had evidently come to terms with the infection, but may well have been the source and passed it on to their children.

I remember one or two of these cases in particular. One was a young man in his early twenties, with a very refined face and obviously of gentle birth. He was in a small terraced house, and was looked after devotedly by a married woman who had I know started her life 'in service'. He was a private patient, and his bills were paid regularly by a firm of solicitors. When he was dying, the woman who looked after him surprised me by asking whether she should send for his relatives — I had always assumed that he had none as no-one had ever been to see him before to my knowledge. I was told that there was a lady who would like to see me if I could arrange to be with the boy at a certain time, and in due course the 'heavily veiled lady' of the Victorian novels was there evidently in deep distress. I had made a point of not observing too closely but she spoke with a gentle and aristocratic accent, and I should imagine that this was his mother.

Another was a splendid old lady who lived to the age of nearly eighty. She had only got one active lung as the other one was completely obliterated by tuberculous fibrosis, and she told me how she developed the disease when she was a bright young girl of seventeen. The doctor had put her to bed, and the treatment at that time was to seal up the windows and not allow the slightest breath of fresh air into a room which was always kept heated even in summer time. After many years of this existence she remembered the incredible day when Dr Tench came in and threw the window wide open and said, 'My dear, the new treatment is to give you as much fresh air as possible!' As well as having survived the pulmonary tuberculosis, she was even luckier in living through one of Dr Tench's operations for what I take to have been an appendix abscess. For the actual operation she was taken down to what used to be the work-house, the grim Victorian pile which has now been divided up into a rabbit warren of flats. There she was chloro-formed by the old assistant, and Dr Tench drained the abscess which then formed what appeared to be a permanent fistula. This only healed after a matter of a dozen years or so, during which time it drained faecal and purulent matter. Yet when I knew her she was a most cheerful old thing, deeply religious, and very grateful for small attentions and a regular visit every two or three weeks.

The case of the boy with the veiled relation reminds me of another patient, a man of about sixty who lodged in part of a farmhouse. He suffered from tertiary syphilis, and a very persistent urethral stricture which I had to dilate with bougies every week. Inevitably he suffered from urinary infection, against which we had no very effective treatment, as this was long before the discovery of antibiotics. He was a cultured man who had been well educated and his room

59

was lined with Greek and Latin classical authors from which I would often find him reading: and he took some pleasure in teasing me, who was supposed to have had a classical education, with quotations which were literally Greek to me. Again his accounts were paid by a London firm of solicitors, and the farmer's wife with whom he lodged used to hint that he went under an assumed name.

A row of cottages called Bellhouse Villas beld several of my old friends. In one of them there was Mrs Joyce who was a chronic invalid, when I took over from Dr Tench she was a bit over fifty years old. I introduced myself to her and she said, 'Oh, you needn't bother about me too much, doctor, I shan't be here long with you', and for thirty-seven years we waged a more or less friendly battle: her usual reply to my greeting of, 'Well, how are you today?' was 'Oh, doctor, did you want to kill me?' and then she continued with the frightful things that my last medicine or tablets had done to her stomach, her joints and other parts of her body. This was the opening gambit from which our play developed; I usually saw her once a month and she looked forward enormously to the battle. When I finally went to say goodbye on retirement from the N.H.S. I reminded her of our first conversation and she gave a high pitched cackle and said, 'Yes, I reckon I'll see your next young doctor out too!'

Her brother was always very keen to hear how I had done when out hunting, and whether I was coming to the meet at High Easter. Fifty years ago he had been earth stopper to the then Master and he said there was always a fox either in Dobbs or Callis coverts. He said, 'You see, doctor, he told me about a fortnight before they were going to draw these coverts, so I used to get an old tom-cat and knock it on the head and hang it up in a sack in my shed. The night before they were coming, I'd go down and stop the earths, and I'd nail that cat by the tail about five foot up a tree in the middle of the little copse. Well they say a fox can smell a vixen ten miles away, and I reckon they could smell that old tom-cat twice as far so there was always one or two foxes hanging round scrapping at that tree trying to get at it. There's nothing an old fox likes better than a good high tom-cat.'

In another cottage lived an old lady who suffered from severe diabetes. She was a fat old thing and very cheerful in spite of gangrenous toes which had to be amputated one by one: and she regularly went into a diabetic coma on Thursday evenings. It took me a little time to realise that it was always on Thursday, but I found no reason as to why it should be that particular day because both she and the younger sister with whom she lived assured me that she never deviated from her diet and was very strict. I certainly doubted this, but at the same time there seemed no clue until one day I was talking to a friend at a drinks party and she told me how much she enjoyed doing the 'meals on wheels'. Quite by chance she mentioned this old lady who looked forward to her visits on Thursday with great enthusiasm, especially when she had meat pie followed by suet roll and golden syrup. When I taxed the old lady with her disgraceful behaviour she replied, 'But oh, doctor, I used to ask her if that was all right for me to have it, and she said: "Bless you, my dear, it'll do you a lot of good."' I asked her whether she had told the van lady that she was a diabetic, and she replied innocently but rather smugly, 'Oh, but didn't she know, doctor?' and looked me straight in the eye.

If you live and practice in a neighbourhood for long enough, houses become identified in your mind with what has happened in them — births, illness, tragedy, death and bereavement, because the doctor's association with his patients is on the whole on unhappy occasions and it is the sadness which tends to stand out most in his mind.

One farmhouse has a sad memory for me. There was a very attractive young family of half a dozen children with a young mother and father there, and in the summer of the early 1930s there was an epidemic of diarrhoea and sickness in the neigbourhood.

One afternoon when I was out at the surgery at High Easter I had a message to say that they were all down with it and would I go and see them and if possible take something along with me, so I mixed up a large bottle of chalk and opium, and saw the children who all seemed fairly bright: I told the mother the various doses to give and to let me know if they didn't get on.

Some ten days later the mother came down to the surgery and said they'd all got well except for one little girl of about eight years old. She still seemed very poorly and would I go and look at her. To my horror I found that she had an acute peritonitis with signs of an abscess in her pelvis.

The surgeon in Chelmsford, a general practitioner, said that if I brought her straight in he could do what was possible provided I would give the anaesthetic, so I drove mother and child to Chelmsford and within an hour's time he had drained half a pint of creamy white pus from her abdomen: but it was a forlorn hope and the child died a few days later. It looked as though this had been lit up by the epidemic, or had just occurred at the same time and so been missed.

There is a small cottage on an isolated green up at Tilty where I had to see an old farm worker who lived there with his middle-aged daughter. He told me a sad story. He had lived in that cottage ever since he got married some forty years before, and he was happy with a wife whom he loved dearly and three small children. One summer day the farmer asked him if he would like a lift in to the fair at Chelmsford where he was taking his other farm workers for a treat, and they thoroughly enjoyed themselves. The peak of the visit was an Italian ice-cream stall, something which they had never tasted before.

A fortnight later he said he had buried his wife and two of his children, all dead from the diphtheria which they had caught (so the doctor said, and along with several others in the neighbourhood of Chelmsford) from the Italian ice-cream.

There is a farmhouse where both husband and wife died under my care. I knew the wife fairly well when I had to go and look after her family, but she never seemed to have anything wrong with herself until one day when she asked to examine her and I found that she had a large and inoperable carcinoma of the uterus. I asked her why ever she had not come to me before, as she must have realised something serious was wrong. Her reply was, 'Doctor, you know that farming is doing badly. We like to pay our bills, and I won't come to the doctor unless I'm sure there really is something the matter.' In fact this was not an uncommon thing to happen, but they did not always die as surely as she did some short time later. Some years later he died, still quite young, from a 'coronary'.

There is a happy association with one house. A wealthy young couple just got married before my wife and I did, and we saw quite a little bit of them socially. One day the young wife developed appendicitis, and the husband said that I must get a London specialist down. So I rang up my old surgical chief and he told me to get one of the rooms ready as an operating theatre; he would be down within three hours with all the necessary paraphernalia. In due course two Daimler hire cars arrived, with the surgeon and the sister in the first one, two nurses in the second one, and the two drivers acted as porters. A collapsible operating table was strapped on the roof of one of the cars, and within half-an-hour of his arrival we were removing a perfectly straightforward acute appendix. Anaesthetics in those days were given by the simple 'rag and bottle' method, a mixture of chloroform and ether on an open mask. I sent the girl off to sleep happily because when I put the mask over her face I apologised for getting her eyelashes in it, and said they were quite the longest ones I had ever seen.

Early in the 1930s a local farmer developed retention of urine. I relieved him by a catheter but advised him that he ought to have his prostate gland removed. He saw a consultant in London and arranged for this, but just before he went into hospital he asked me, 'Doctor, shall I be any good afterwards, with girls I mean?' I told him that I simply didn't know, it was not a question that I had discussed with any of the rather elderly patients whom I had seen in hospital: and in those days sex life was not usually discussed by doctors anyway. 'Well, doctor, I hope it will be all right; you see, four year-old horses and fourteen-year-old girls are all I'm interested in nowadays.' I did not know this man very well, and this explained a good deal. The door used to be opened by a rather grim faced woman whom I took to be his house-keeper, but who turned out to be his wife who hardly spoke and who kept very much in the background. He was a dapper little man with a stiff collar and a bow tie, usually in riding breeches and very much in evidence in the local horsy world.

He had his operation and came home and had an un-eventful convalescence. The next spring I was standing at a point-to-point looking at the horses in the paddock when I noticed that I was standing next to him. We discussed the runners, he doing so with considerable inside knowledge and then he said, 'Oh by the way, doctor, I've quite got over that operation now: I'm riding them again, thank God — both kinds!'

CHAPTER V

MATERNITY

Before the National Health Service in 1948, each town or village had a nursing association to which each member subscribed weekly. There was a committee responsible for collecting the subscriptions, and for engaging the nurse and providing a house and car for her. She was a very important part of the community, and often acted as a stepping-stone to the doctor. As she lived in the village, which might be some distance from Dunmow, people would consult her to make sure whether it was necessary for the doctor to visit the patient: and a good district nurse who had the confidence of the doctor was of the greatest use.

Medical training at that time did not include the practice of medicine outside the hospital, so that it was quite a surprise for any young doctor in his first practice to know that district nurses even existed. But one was bound to meet them very soon, and I met mine a few days after I began work. It was a dark November evening, and I was sent for to see a gypsy in difficult labour out near Aythorpe Roding. I arrived at a very poor little encampment which consisted of two or three tents not more than four feet high along the ridge, and seven or eight feet long. There were one or two bicycles or prams but no caravans, and the usual small crowd of ragged children and barking dogs. I was taken to the tent where the woman lay, and told that the nurse was inside with her: but all I could see was a pair of very stout black boots poking out of the opening of the tent, continued up with serviceable black stockings. I told the nurse I was coming in, but she said, 'There's only room for one of us, doctor, so I'll come out' so my first introduction to a nurse was her nether half emerging into the damp twilight. She was a good friend for many years, and taught me a great deal of midwifery under primitive conditions.

The payment for confinement was at the rate of three guineas for the doctor if he was there when the baby was born but only two if he arrived afterwards: and time and again I have arrived to find the nurse pushing the baby back as hard as mum was trying to push it out, and saying as I opened the door, 'Oh, doctor, I've just managed to hold it up for you' and letting it come out like a cricket ball into the wicket keeper's hands. Other times she would be apologetic and say she had done her best to hold it up but it insisted on coming. My attitude was that the best babies arrived without the doctor but I gather Dr Tench used to grumble if he missed the extra guinea.

There was a popular superstition that 'raspberry leaf tea' would make labour easier, and young wives were encouraged by their mothers to drink it regularly as their time got nearer; if all went well, the tea and grandma were given the credit.

One of my last recollections of district nurses is a very happy one. There was a big snowstorm and all the roads were blocked for a day or two so that doctors could not get out to High Easter at all. Two nurses had lived together for many years helping each other and working on a rota system: they were excellent nurses, but both of them were little women and one often wondered how they managed to manhandle some of their rather bulky patients.

One of them particularly wanted to visit a mother who had recently had a baby, but couldn't get through the snow drifts: word got round and four rough young farm workers from the neighbouring cottages who were idle because of the snow presented themselves at her door and said, 'Come along, nurse, we'll carry you there!' and they did. She told them: 'You're all my babies, I was there when each one of you was born.'

When I first came to practise the nurses dressed in a dark blue uniform with a rather imposing felt hat on the top of it, and it was many years before I persuaded one of the nurses to take off her hat when she was conducting a confinement. It used to be said that the first sight that greeted any of the small inhabitants of Dunmow was her hat, and that accounted for quite a lot of things in later life!

Once we had unexpected triplets, before the young wives accepted the custom of antenatal care. The district nurse sent for me because she was not happy about the case: she was a biggish young woman with a large abdomen and nurse and I were surprised when baby arrived, how small it was, it must have been under four pounds, and the mother's abdomen looked much the same size as before. It was obvious that there was another one to come and we both expected quite a large twin, but no, another small

65

instalment arrived; then finally the third.

There was no baby unit at Chelmsford, and the nearest incubator was in London: the ambulance service was negligible, and the mother was unwilling to part with the babies even if we could have persuaded a London hospital to take them. So the nurse and a neighbour did their best with artificial milk and fountain pen fillers, and each baby had its own hot water bottle underneath the pillow it was laid on. They did very well at first, but I was doubtful about the outcome and advised the mother to have them baptised. We christened them Matthew, Mark and Luke, but it was the middle of a hot summer and gastro-enteritis was widespread in the neighbourhood. Inevitably they caught it and died quite quickly. However the mother subsequently raised a large family, but in single doses after that.

Until the war brought the emergency hospitals in a ring between thirty and forty miles from London, the nearest maternity department was a very small one, thirteen miles away at Chelmsford. There was no consultant, and to get a good opinion one had to rely on specialists in London. On a foggy night in November I had a patient in labour who had old rheumatic myocarditis, a serious heart condition: I had previously decided that she was going to have twins, but as she was a fairly large woman I did not anticipate great difficulty with them: however her labour was prolonged and she seemed to be making no progress, so I rang up a consultant in London who said he would come down. It was in the very early days of the war and the blackout restrictions for motor cars were very tightly applied, there was thick fog, and the journey from London to Dunmow was a matter of forty miles. From there it was some seven miles on to the patient's home. The consultant had never been out into this part of the world before, and I felt that this was a case where the police might reasonably be asked to help. And help they did, most efficiently. Police cars guided my consultant from his home right to my surgery in a matter of about two hours. From there I took him on and he saw the case with me.

After he had examined the patient, his opinion was not reassuring for he had difficulty over the vaginal examination owing to the patient being very fat, the bed very low and soft and the tissues hardened through pressure of prolonged labour. He thought that there might be an abnormal baby, an encephalic monster.

He decided that we must try at once to get the child out, and I proceeded to give the patient an anaesthetic. Remember that I had no oxygen with me, and the anaesthetic was given by dropping a mixture of chloroform and ether on to an open mask with a preceding dose of 'twilight sleep' (an injection of morphine and hyoscine). Under the anaesthetic it was easier for the specialist to examine her, and what had seemed to be the headless end of the monster turned out to be its opposite end; in fact he had been putting his finger right up into its backside! Delivery was fairly easy with the first twin, and he was then able to put forceps on to the head of the second one, and we had two fine boys who survived to be a most frightful headache in due course to their parents.

Nearly all my young married couples wanted to start a family pretty soon, and certainly their parents watched anxiously and often did their little bit with suitable decorations in the young couple's bedroom. Along with the text worked in cross-stitch there might be the nearest thing to a pornographic picture that the local stationers could supply, Gibson girls and rather coy half dressed ladies: but the statuary was much franker, and bedside lights of naked and alluring girls used to be placed strategically to stimulate the young husband. I noticed that these were more common when the wife was what we call 'homely' in her looks.

If there seemed to be delay in becoming pregnant, then the old mums used to advise the young wife after intercourse to lie quite still on her back with her buttocks supported high in the air by a pile of pillows, and they even went so far as to tell the husband to tie her feet up to the bedpost which was sometimes present in those days.

I suppose the oldest game played by married couples during pregnancy is guessing the sex of the baby. In many cases a succession of just boys or just girls prompted the question to the doctor as to whether there was anything they could do about it. In the early 1930s there was an eminent gynaecologist who claimed that he could do just this; I read his article, and so I went up to see him. He explained that as the sex was entirely decided by the sperm which are equally divided into male-bearing and female-bearing kinds, anything one could do to encourage one or discourage the other was going to be effective. He thought that a slightly acid reaction favoured the female-bearing sperm, and a slightly alkaline one favoured the male.

As all his patients seemed to want boys, and I gather that this included quite a number of aristocracy who had so far not produced male heirs but a succession of little girls who all needed dowries, the lucrative part of his practice was to try to produce these boys: so he advised the mothers to douche themselves with a weak solution of sodium bicarbonate before trying for the next infant. He also took the reaction of the vaginal moisture at various times during the monthly cycle, from which he could say when it tended to be more alkaline and finally he made them take a bicarbonate of soda tablet three or four times a day. He admitted that he had been known sometimes to guard against failure by putting the opposite sex on the patient's notes so as to have something to produce with an angry parent!

I tried it a very few times, and I remember certainly two successes. One was for a girl where there had so far been boys, and the other one rather overdid it because the mother already had three girls, and when boy twins turned up she wasn't as pleased as she might have been.

CHAPTER VI

CONTACTS WITH THE LAW

In cases of sudden death G.P.s were expected to do their own post mortems in the nearest convenient building to where the body was found, usually somewhere in the village where the person had lived. In Dunmow there was no regular post mortem room until Dr Francis Camps (later a famous pathologist) arranged for one to be built in the early thirties. People were not too keen on having it done in their own house, so that it usually had to be done in an outhouse or barn with water supplied in buckets, slop basins for the dirty water and soiled towels. Light was provided by oil lamps, or if one was lucky with a Tilley pressure paraffin lamp raided from the local pub which usually had one.

Suicides always had to have a post mortem done, even though the cause of death was pretty obvious. Drowning was a favourite method for depressed farmers and farm labourers, and I can think of three quite small ponds where unfortunate people have ended their lives; in one case there were only five inches of water. There was one case where a man used a water butt. He was a butcher who had got into financial difficulties, and his wife couldn't find him one morning so she sent her son out into the yard to look for him. The weedy teenager hunted high and low until he finally saw a pair of boots sticking out of the water butt: the unfortunate man was pulled out with some difficulty.

I can think of three hangings; in one case the man had carefully removed his false teeth and balanced them on the handle of the wheelbarrow on to which he had climbed before jumping off, and they were undisturbed. One youngish man was found hanging in an outhouse: I sent him in an ambulance to the new mortuary of a neighbouring hospital where the pathologist surprisingly said that this probably was an accident during a sexual fantasy orgy. Underneath his ordinary clothes the man had got on some of his wife's foundation garments, in his pocket book there were pornographic photographs, and there was fresh semen in his penis and on his underclothes. The pathologist thought that he was in the habit of partially strangling himself to produce an orgasm, and on this occasion had allowed it to go too far.

The first winter I was here, I was not yet engaged: so that I had many invitations from the mothers of suitable unmarried daughters. One was to a hunt ball around Christmas time, and I climbed into my tails, customary in those days. As I was setting off, I had a message that a body had been found in a ditch at High Easter, and that the policeman would wait in the pub until I came to do a post mortem so that he could report it to the coroner. There was snow and a heavy frost, and the village pump was frozen. The policeman told me that he had succeeded in getting me two buckets of water and had commandeered the pub Tilley lamp, which gave good enough light to reveal the coronary clot which I expected and found in time to be only a few minutes late for dinner.

Recently there was a case in the newspapers of a body in the mortuary which was found to be alive, and resuscitated successfully in the hospital. The fear of being buried while still alive was by no means uncommon, and I found that it was quite a usual thing to be asked by relatives, and sometimes by an elderly patient, to be sure to 'open a vein' before a corpse was allowed to be buried. There was a fee for this of two guineas, which was quite a lot of money then and a welcome bonus for work which was not very well paid.

There used to be a great many more tramps in the thirties than are seen nowadays; they tended to establish themselves in deserted farm buildings or cottages, of which there were quite a large number at that time when farming was probably at its lowest ebb in this century. Occasionally one would die, and his body sometimes would not be discovered for several days: a policeman would then have to find a doctor to go out and inspect the body before informing the coroner. Just as rats leave a sinking ship, fleas will desert a corpse for the nearest human: so that I used to take a bottle of chloroform with me, and the policeman and I would liberally anoint ourselves with it round our neck and wrists and trousers which we would tuck into our socks. In order to be sure there were no marks of external injuries, one had to undress the corpse, and once in a deserted barn in Little Dunmow one could see the fleas hopping as we took off the rags which the poor chap had been wearing.

Next morning I drove up into the town, and the policeman on point duty at the crossroads by the Saracen's Head was more than usually animated in his direction of the traffic. With one arm he waved cars on, and with the other one he surreptitiously scratched his crutch vigorously. As I drew up beside him, I also took my hand off the gear lever and scratched in the same place, saying to him out of the window, 'Yes, we both forgot that way in.'

My first experience of being called by the police to examine a drunken driver was not for the driver of a motor car, but for a steam tractor. Between the two world wars, ploughing was often done by a steam plough: this was a big reversible plough pulled by a steel hawser between two traction engines, one at each end of the field. When the plough had finished one furrow, both engines moved on a little, the plough was tipped the other way, and the far engine pulled it back again.

This involved two engines, the plough, a water cart, and a caravan on wheels in which the ploughing men lived, and the team used to travel from one farm to another as the bookings decreed, all linked together as a road train. On this particular Saturday a job had been finished near Cambridge and the whole train was travelling to a farm near Chelmsford to begin after the weekend: at lunchtime the driver stopped at the Swan at Thaxted, where he settled down for a well earned drink or two at the end of a hard week's work. Unfortunately the train was on a slope near the church, and gravity slowly started it downhill, and it only came to a violent stop when it demolished one of the local buses.

The driver was traced back to the Swan, and he ran down to turn off the steam in the engine before collapsing on his back under the machine from where he was extracted by a police car and driven into Dunmow and I was summoned to examine. He was a man of about 60, in good health, and extremely drunk.

The firm which owned the ploughing team employed counsel at the quarter sessions in Chelmsford, and I appeared to give evidence. I was cross-examined by a very shrewd and experienced barrister, who said he only wanted to ask me one or two quite simple questions. He produced a well-known standard medical textbook, and asked me whether I acknowledged its authority which I did:

whereupon he proceeded to read on the subject of alcoholism, how difficult it was to distinguish it from a whole host of medical conditions. He asked me whether I agreed that this was so, and I did. He then said, 'Doctor Barber, are you quite sure that the driver was suffering from alcoholism and not from one of these conditions?' I said that I was and that concluded my cross-examination.

When it came to his speech for the defence, he paid tribute to my thorough examination of the patient, but continued — 'He is sure, where the authorities say that it is difficult.' And of course the jury found the driver not guilty. The barrister came up to me outside, patted me on the shoulder, and said, 'My dear fellow, I was so sorry, but it really was child's play.'

I have told earlier on of the wealthy bachelor who got me out in the early hours of the morning, but there was another patient of mine whom I had to see on more than one occasion in a police station where he had habit of telephoning me to say that he would wait for examination by the police doctor until I arrived. On one foggy night I got there and watched the local G.P. do a very cursory examination, after which he left. But I said that I would like to do one further test, and asked for the loan of the office typewriter. Now this patient was a part-time journalist for a well-known newspaper, and I told him that it was important that he should write at my dictation without making a single mistake, and that as it was a strange typewriter to him he could of course go as slowly as he liked. I then dictated — 'I, so and so, am writing this to show that I am in full command of my faculties,' and so on: when he had done this, taking his time of course, I got the sergeant to countersign it, put it in my pocket and we left.

When his case came up, his counsel offered no evidence except to produce this piece of paper, as something that actually was written at the time. He had no difficulty in getting my patient off.

Acute mental disease in general practice is nearly always dramatic. It involved certifying the patient when he or she goes over the border line; this usually occurs suddenly, and creates a great disturbance in the neighbourhood until the necessary steps are taken to remove the patient to a mental hospital.

Before the present Act, a patient had to be certified and

this meant getting hold of the Relieving Officer (who later became the Mental Welfare Officer) and a Justice of the Peace.

The acute situation seems to happen more often at night; it may be because the patient tends to become more disturbed in the dark, or that his failure to quieten down and go to sleep rouses the family's desperation so that they send for the doctor: it certainly was usually a matter of getting the Relieving Officer and the J.P. out of bed.

Late one Saturday night just after the war I was sent for to see a French woman who was staying with relatives on an isolated village green, and it turned out that she was being allowed out of a mental hospital for the weekend. This hospital was the other side of London, so that it meant certifying her afresh: there was one elderly sporting farmer who lived quite close who was a J.P. so I naturally rang him up. He replied from his bed that he had never certified a patient before so he was afraid he couldn't help me: but I said that in that case it was high time he did and insisted that he should come, which he did with a very bad grace. Meanwhile the patient thought she was back in France in the Resistance, where I gather she had been very active, and evidently had had a bad time as a result; and this was a strong factor in her mental condition. When the J.P. walked in, she looked very hard at him and said in a steely voice, 'Have a cigarette', to which he replied rather jovially 'No thanks, I don't smoke', whereupon she exclaimed 'Aha, I knew it. A policeman! Look at his boots! I will get even with you but I refuse to say another word.' My J.P. backed hurriedly away into another room, signed where we showed him and was out of the house like a shot. When he had gone she calmed down, and was persuaded quite easily to get into the ambulance and to go off with the Mental Welfare Officer, who told me that she had behaved very well in the ambulance and on her arrival at Severalls hospital. There she was interviewed by the young doctor on duty, and answered his questions pleasantly: but when she got up to go with the night sister to her ward, she snatched up a huge glass inkwell from the desk, hurled it at the doctor and made a bolt for the door.

Several of the houses in the neighbourhood are reputed to be haunted. One of them is a large Elizabethan house which used to be very tumbledown and divided into three or

73

four parts with farm workers or sometimes just squatters living there. It was an eerie place, ill-kept and overgrown, damp and draughty: it certainly was a very suitable place for ghosts. One of the labourers was about fifty, and he had often been 'queer', but he was especially affected at the full moon, when he had the habit of becoming deeply religious, going into the overgrown garden, praying loudly and singing hymns. This used to be tolerated by his family and the neighbours, until he insisted that prayers could only be said while stark naked, and he had to be certified under these conditions twice: on one occasion he gave us the slip, so that all of us, J.P., Mental Welfare Officer, doctor, family and other residents, had to join in a glorious moonlight game of hide and seek with the naked madman.

Twenty years later this house was bought by a local farmer and completely renovated into a most attractive home. His wife's mother was living with them; she was a very old lady whom I had known ever since I came to Dunmow. She had a failing heart and was on regular digitalis. I was away one night when she became feverish and slightly delirious, and Dr Walford from Felsted came to see her: he had not visited her before, but he settled her down and I saw her next day. She said to me, 'Your partner came to see me last night, I thought he was a charming man, but very odd. Why did he bring all those black dancing girls with him?'

CHAPTER VII

WARTIME

War was declared on a bright Sunday morning, September 3rd 1939. No sooner was Chamberlain's speech finished than the air raid sirens sounded their warning; it was the first of many false alarms, but we were not to know that: the eerie undulating wail of that first time sent a shiver through everyone, with a reaction of 'Goodness, they have been quick to start.' Nothing happened. Half an hour later the 'all clear' was sounded.

The next night was less happy: the siren sounded the air raid warning at about eight o'clock in the evening so the whole household moved into the corridor behind the drawing room leading to the consulting room which was in the middle of the house with no exterior walls. The siren had unfortunately broken after sounding the alarm and was unable to sound the 'all clear', which we would have heard as it was only two hundred yards away. The wardens sounded the 'all clear' with hand bells, but we did not hear them and so spent an uncomfortable night. The only other time the siren failed to sound the 'all clear' during the war was when it was put out of action by a German bomb.

A year before we knew we were on the brink of war, and for a long time before that we had been warned that it was inevitable and told to get ready before it was too late. Rather half-heartedly Air Raid Protection had been organised, with drills, air raid shelters dug, Anderson shelters (a sort of glorified dog kennel) had been installed, and plans for evacuation for the large towns, and of medical services, had been drawn up. Perhaps the pace of life had accelerated a little bit, a general feeling of enjoy it while we can; we had bought more clothes and tins of food and replaced saucepans which were wearing out, but with the feeling that it might never happen. Now that we were actually at war it came almost as a relief; we knew where we were, and could get on with the serious business.

That first air raid warning was interesting in that it showed how people would react to such emergencies. With my wife and myself there were two children, a boy of 7 and a girl of 5, two maids, a nurse and a nursemaid; the latter did not live in; as well as a gardener and an occasional boy. The children and I think to a lesser degree the two maids, tended to take their cue from us: the odd one out was Nanny who panicked hysterically from the first sound of the sirens. It was no fault of hers, simply the way she was made, but we could not have an unpredictable in the house and she had to go. It was interesting to see the remains of her influence on Philippa, who had been 'Nannyed' more than we had realised. The children used to have their meals in the nursery, but now mostly fed with us, and we found that Nanny had allowed and perhaps even encouraged fads and likes and dislikes in food, clothes and way of life that were becoming fixed habits. Poor Philippa had a short sharp desensitising course which psychiatrists might say was highly traumatic to a growing child, but in a wartime household it was obvious that she would have to conform on the surface: so that when she announced that she did not like marmalade it was quite simple — she need not have it. My wife complained that she made an endless fuss about the order in which she did things when she went to bed, so I volunteered to take it on one evening. I am afraid I got her properly muddled, by making her do everything in such a wrong order, saying her prayers in the middle of her bath, then brushing her teeth before she dried, that we heard no more about that. She always had beautiful curls, but once Nanny had gone her hair reverted to its straight natural wave and nothing more.

The maids slept in the attic at the top of the house, and when the siren started sounding at night, they trooped downstairs to the shelter, first of all to the cellar (they didn't do that twice) and finally to the front consulting room. I told them that I couldn't have them running upstairs and down at all times of the night, and for heaven's sake decide where they would like to sleep once the air raid had sounded, and bed down there for the rest of the war. They did this happily, and slept downstairs, bringing their bedclothes down each evening. On the other hand we decided to stay upstairs, and of course the children stayed with us. Some years later when the flying bombs began to come over we could lie in bed and watch the flickering light away to the north through the big window of our bedroom, and when the rump... rump... rump... stopped we used to count twelve until the bang and say 'Thank goodness, that's another one that has missed London.' Dunmow is such an insignificant pimple on the map, of no possible military importance, that any enemy activity from the air could only be accidental, and our siren merely was one of a great chain sounding in unison, along with important industrial centres such as Chelmsford where the Hoffman ball-bearing factory was very severely bombed in the blitz, as well as the Marconi works and the railway junction, but that was fifteen miles away, and any bombs around us were unloaded by chance on the way home.

After that first day and the shock of the air raid alarm life went on much as usual. Until the invasion of Europe in May 1940, there was a period that we used to call the 'phoney war': Germany was occupied on the Eastern Front endeavouring to crush Russia before she turned on the West, so we carried on normally, and even began to wonder if anything would really happen before it was all over. There were scattered air raids; one on a near by airfield at Debden was a noisy affair, and as I insisted on going down the garden to feed the hens whether there was an alert or not, I had to pacify Daphne by putting on my white ARP tin hat as I carried the food down. There were tales of lone enemy aircraft flying low over the fields and machine-gunning cattle and stray agricultural labourers, so that when I was out shooting one day in October with Daphne and Whisky at Brook End along the Braintree Road, I had reluctantly to climb into a ditch when aircraft came over although they usually turned out to be ours. All the doctors had been enrolled in the ARP, and worked on a rota basis for calls at night. Later when night raids became regular and serious we used to have to go up and sleep at the Foakes Hall for the nights on duty. At the same time an Observer Corps was enrolled; men and women were trained to identify the types of aircraft so as to distinguish between friends and enemies. A post was set up at the top of the mill in St Edmunds Lane in the house belonging to Mr Davey: it was manned throughout the 24 hours, and all aircraft were reported by telephone to the police station.

Before the beginning of the war the evacuees were organised. All children from London were given the opportunity of being housed in the country and a large proportion accepted this. As time went on they tended to drift back but each house in Dunmow was allotted a certain number. As a doctor's house we were let off, but Daphne volunteered for two, and on September 1st, two days *before* war was actually declared, they arrived.

I remember that the evacuees first came to the Foakes Memorial Hall where they had labels tied on them in different colours. One colour was for bedwetters, one for verminous (scabies) and one for headlice or ringworm: these tended to get left to the last because the householders came and were allotted a certain amount of choice for the first comers. As we had our own two children it did not seem a great effort to take two of about the same age, and the two little boys who came seemed clean and docile. We introduced them to the garden and to our children, but they did not think much of that: the older boy showed some initiative in chasing the dog round with a bow and arrow, and when he was stopped they installed themselves on the doorstep of the front door with just the narrow pavement between them and the busy street. From that point of vantage they exchanged shouted conversation with their friends, not at all inhibited as to their opinions of their respective homes. When it came to mealtimes their manners were of course different from ours: once when we gave them kippers they solemnly picked the bones out of their mouths and scraped their fingers on the polished edge of the table to get them off. Although we provided them with two beds, one was never slept in, and the other one was always sopping wet. We fed them as best we could, and we were put properly in our place when after a few days their parents came down to take them out for the day, laden with sticky buns which they gorged before they had even left the house, and after what we had thought was quite a substantial midday meal. As no bombs were dropped on London, the parents quite wisely took them back after only six weeks, and we felt we had done our duty!

But we had quite a lot of spare room, and in November troops moved in to the neighbourhood for training. They were regular regiments, the 60th Rifles and the Rifle Brigade: their headquarters were at the Saracen's Head opposite, and we volunteered to give beds to two officers, who would go across for meals to the Mess in the hotel. The visitors book shows a series of these officers for two years; they were regular soldiers, charming, polite and often highly cultured. Several stand out; we started with an enormous tall captain and another whom I don't remember, but they came from different regiments, so that as they dressed up in mess dress every night, their batmen would attend to give them their baths, put them into their mess dress, and then stay down in the kitchen to the disruption of the maids' routine until their lords and masters returned from mess when they would take them out of their kit. I suggested once that one batmen should stay to do both of them, and this was apparently such an apalling idea that I hastily withdrew it. They looked beautiful in their 'blues' with silver chains on their shoulders, and highly polished buttons and spotless half wellingtons and spurs. The following June they went to France and were left behind to cover the evacuation of Dunkirk: all except one were killed or taken prisoner in the defence of Calais.

That winter was a particularly severe one with long periods of snow and ice; the troops training had a bad time as they were mostly mechanised, and on one occasion twelve motor cyclists out of twelve failed to return from an exercise. The roads were icy, and byroads were not sanded: both my motor cars were put out of action in one black week. The first was a Hillman in which I was on my way to Felsted, and I saw in the distance an army truck being driven much too fast and skidding from side to side. I had to pass it in quite a narrow road so I decided to stop and get out of the car and take cover in a ditch: as I opened the door I realised I had little hope of standing on the slippery surface, so I hastily got back, shut the door and waited for the inevitable head-on collision. When it came it lifted the car several feet backwards, pushing the engine out into the chassis — in peacetime it would have been a write-off. I got the name of the officer commanding the particular unit, and then put in the usual channels for a new car, to be greeted with the news that no new cars were being issued to civilians under any circumstances whatever. I went to see the officer and told him my tale of woe. He listened sympathetically, and he replied:

'That's very lucky for you, because I happen to be a director of Rootes. You've already been told we can't give you a new car, but if you would ask your garage for a complete list of the parts they will need, I will see personally that they are supplied as quickly as may be.' He was as good as his word, and in due course the car was completely rebuilt and went on to give splendid service throughout the war. On the outbreak of war I had brought it brand new because I had a feeling that we should not be seeing any more new ones until the war was ended.

Within a week of that accident, another army vehicle came out of a side turning much too fast and collided with my Wolseley. Here I was only slightly damaged, but his vehicle was out of action with a broken radiator. It was a different unit, and I got in touch with the commanding officer right away: he was very angry, as nearly all his men had been in accidents recently; he called the driver up in front of me, and said:

'You know what I said last time, that if there was another accident all leave would be stopped, not only for you, but for the whole unit. That will now happen until this doctor's car is back on the road.'

When the driver had left, he turned to me and said: 'They'll take it out of him.'

Ration cards had been prepared in advance, and were now issued although we did not have to use them for some little time. At first it was merely for meat and sugar, but as time went on fats and sweets were included, and a different book was issued for clothes and shoes. Every so often we were told what the coupons represented, and it was progressively less and less as the war went on.

Gas masks were issued early in the war. We shall never know whether this serious preparation had any effect on the policy of the German High Command, but gas was never used. There were plenty of alarms, and old ladies were constantly telephoning the police at night to assure them that IT had come at last. A worried sergeant finally appealed to me to go out late at night to a cottage at Canfield to an elderly woman in hysterics: and the police were equally worried by constant reports of 'spies'. Lights reported at night were as often as not ordinary railway signals seen from a new angle; where there was anyone with a foreign name or known to be of German or Italian extraction, neighbours were constantly on the lookout for suspicious movements. For the issue of gas masks we queued up in the Foakes Hall and were fitted and shown how to wear them: we were advised to put them on at least once a day, and to become accustomed to doing household chores in them: but few people persevered for more than a day or two. Later on in an ARP exercise we were made to wear them for three hours on end at night, and it fell to me as the doctor to drive an ambulance to Saffron Walden in one. By the grace of God we got there, mainly because there was so little traffic.

Petrol rationing came in early — there were a few gallons for each month, with supplementary coupons for essential work such as doctors and regular services; dustmen, post and food delivery, and of course for farmers. I had no complaints, they never queried a doctor's needs: I soon learnt to time my visits to combine with other things, on Saturdays there was always somebody to see in the neighbourhood of one of my shoots; a few distant patients could be combined with shopping and even in summer with the pool at Braintree. I would announce to the children that I had to visit Mrs Smith beyond Rayne, in good time for them to collect their friends, and an awe-inspiring crowd of young hopefuls would gather in the drive in the afternoon equipped with towels and bathers. I had a large Wolseley, and they crammed in, reminding me of the stunt of seeing how many students could get into a telephone kiosk. I remember once counting them as they got out and to my disbelief arrived at a figure of 17!

Our officers were settling in and we adapted to this new way of life, and then one Sunday afternoon the front door bell rang and the maid came out into the garden where I was busily digging to announce that there was an officer and a lady who wished to see me in the drawing room. The Captain and his wife were in their best clothes — she was actually wearing a veil! They asked me whether I could possibly put them up: he was quite frank in telling me that one of his brother officers had told him I had a small empty room; they were desperate to sleep somewhere and could we put them up until they found something more permanent. Of course Daphne said yes, and they stayed for several months. They were dears, and became friends — we visited them in Ireland after the war: an ulterior motive in choosing us was the fact that she was having a threatened miscarriage. A day or two later the front bell rang again, and Captain C asked me if he I could visit his wife. He was always very correct and if he wanted to talk to me he went outside, rang the door bell and gave a message to the maid: he was relieved when I told him it would be simpler just to look for us himself. The miscarriage was averted, and in due course twins were added to the family in Ireland.

The blackout was a considerable feature of the early war. Wardens paraded the streets at night with strict instructions to call the attention of householders to any chink which was showing. This meant a good deal of fitting black curtains and blinds: we were fortunate at Rood End in having wooden shutters in a row along the front which were completely effective, and upstairs we had roller blinds of black material installed. Each evening there was a ceremonial blacking out and at first one of us used to walk along outside in the street and round the garden to see if any light was showing.

There was a curious incident at Coldharbour in Surrey; Daphne's old home. Like ourselves, her parents opened their house to officers from Princess Patricia's Canadian Light Infantry in the neighbourhood, and they had quite a number sleeping and sometimes feeding there with them. Their terrace commands a wide view of the valley below and stretching away for fifteen to twenty miles in the distance, a lovely view: and a beautiful vantage point for spotting any gleam of light showing in the complete gloom. Most nights a bright light shone at intervals, straight into the sky some miles away, and the officers got quite excited. Bearings were taken, both from their terrace and from further along the ridge so as to be able to get a triangle, narrowing the search to a small bunch of houses. These were kept under constant observation, and in due course the light shone and was spotted as coming from the roof of a large house. The army pounced, only to find their commanding officer in residence; the offending light was traced to his dressing room, where the skylight had escaped notice, and had never been blacked out!

Along with the blackout car lights were a problem and the solution by the authorities was the issue of headlamp masks. These were large black discs with a series of slits which allowed glimmers of light to be thrown on to the road ahead. When there was no moon, or in fog, one was almost totally blind and could only go at a snail's pace. With the window down and guided by the verge I frequently lost my way: as often as not it was because I had forgotten some turning down to a farmyard which I should have crossed instead of following it down until it petered out into a muddy track or even a pond; where did one turn with no reversing lights and squelchy bog on either side? Later when my partner had gone to the war and I had the occasional assistant, it was quite usual for him to have to abandon the car and make his way home as best he could, sometimes even sending for me to fetch him.

ARP, Air Raid Precaution, routine settled down. Regular drills and exercises were held once a week or twice a week, and there was a duty rota under the district wardens. Both Daphne and the dispenser had to don their black helmets with white ARP on them and gumboots and go round at night in their turn, but I think Daphne as a doctor's wife was soon excused. Doctors wore white helmets with black letters on and apart from some general instructions we were not expected to attend anything but the most full-scale exercises.

One result of this full evacuation from London was to benefit this neighbourhood permanently, and that was the formation of emergency medical hospitals in a ring thirty to forty miles round London. Two were built round here, one at Bishops Stortford and the other at Chelmsford: in both cases the existing buildings of old workhouses were taken over and hutted hospitals rapidly added; both have survived until now, nearly fifty years later, and have been established as very useful permanent community hospitals where there was very little before. The entire staff of the Royal Northern Hospital came down to the old Infirmary at Haymeads, which was rechristened the Herts and Essex Hospital, and we enjoyed for the first time in this neighbourhood whole time London consultants with a teaching round open to G.P.s on Wednesday afternoons, and a wonderful atmosphere of keenness and cooperation: the senior physician was also the medical superintendent, Harold Balme, whose influence is still present in the hospital over thirty years later on.

With the E.M.S. hospitals, we had a train load of expectant mothers: these were in special through coaches which came for some reason to Felsted station where they were to get into buses to be taken to improvised maternity wards. I was detailed to meet these ladies, and found myself waiting on the platform, the only male amongst a gang of nurses and lady drivers. They were from the East End and the backchat started with wolf whistles all directed at myself

83

before the train drew up. A whole barrage of questions:

'Good dog racing? Best pubs? Nearest underground? (I'm going straight home). Bookies? I've got a good tip for the 2.30.'

Poor things, they could not understand what an isolated spot they'd arrived at. No buses, no underground, no Sunday trains: I think most of them did stay to have their babies, but they went back as soon as they were able.

The spring of 1940 brought the sudden German turn to the west, the invasion of Norway and Holland and France, and the Blitzkrieg. The phoney war was over and we were rudely awakened. The very ease with which the Germans disregarded the Maginot Line, on which the French had pinned the whole of their defensive policy astonished us and opened our eyes, and the detailed organisation of the Fifth Column throughout the whole of the invading countries brought home to us our own vulnerability. We also had the equivalent of a Maginot Line; the Channel, since the Norman Conquest it had stood between us and invasion from Europe, but we suddenly realised that with the new threat from the air it could now be less secure, and the nation feverishly made good the deficiencies which the invasion of Europe had shown up in our defensive system.

Now we had to consider seriously the question of a shelter away from the house, and we dug one satisfactorily at the bottom of the kitchen garden and covered it with a stout timber frame on the top of which was piled two feet of earth and then the whole lot was turfed over. It might have been of some good against flying debris but would be useless against anything like a direct hit. And I don't think we ever went down there except for practice; but the children and their friends had a lot of fun in it as their private den. But we did bury a corn bin in the floor; this we had filled with tinned food — sardines and bully beef and biscuit tins full of rice, sugar and oatmeal, tins of coffee and tea and cocoa. We forgot all about it until towards the end of the war when we in our turn had invaded Europe; we suddenly remembered this hidden cache of goodies, dug it up and carefully rationed the contents out with great pleasure.

When the Rifle Brigade and the 60th Rifles had been drafted over to France, our spare room was empty once more — but not for long. The fall of France and the desperate evacuation from Dunkirk flooded reception areas in this country. The Saracen's Head was the local depot, Easton Lodge was still standing empty when the Americans came to make the airfield, and when that was full there was still room needed for officers and men while they were being sorted and reorganised into their new units. Again we put the attics at their disposal as an overflow, and the visitors' book shows a stream of officers often for only one or two nights; some we never even saw, for they arrived late and were gone in the morning: one left a note of apology for being so dirty and ashamed to get into the clean sheets: all were grateful. I left quite a few books up there for visitors to browse in and several went missing, but I felt glad that someone had appreciated them.

The rush from Dunkirk was over, and defence lines were being feverishly organised, one of them being the line along the Chelmer river. The staff for this operation moved into the Saracen's Head, and again we provided the overflow: this time to a most charming and cultured regular officer in the Royal Engineers, a Colonel Pemberton, and he stayed with us for the whole time that the line was being constructed and was a most pleasant guest. He brought his wife to stay with him once or twice, and became a great friend of ours and of our children.

About this time our house suffered its only war damage. The road from Bishops Stortford narrows right down opposite my front door, and there is a very small pavement; just room for two cars to pass. Lorries were constantly tearing down the road in convoy, and one night the inevitable happened. I was peacefully lying in my bath before supper, when I felt a distant bump: but as a number of bombs were dropping around the neighbourhood I took no notice and continued to wallow. Later on I heard a hubbub in the street, and idly looked out of the window to see a crowd of people looking at the surgery lower down the road, and on craning my neck out I saw that a lorry had hit the wall fair and square, and its bonnet was embedded in the waiting room. I went down in a dressing gown — it was a fine warm night and my wife tells me that I stayed in that dressing gown for the next three hours. A very worried driver was manoeuvring the lorry out of a hole in the house, with a good deal of noisy advice about what would happen when the support went. An officer arrived obviously fussed, and proceeded to give lots of counter orders. Everybody loved it.

I took the officer indoors to the consulting room, produced a bottle of whisky and said:

'Now what about it?'

'What about what?' he said. 'It'll be repaired in due course, and the War Office will give full compensation.' I replied:

'That waiting room will be used tomorrow by a large number of patients, so we've got to get it repaired right away.'

'Impossible,' he replied. 'I have to get authority.' I telephoned Mr Harris, the local builder, and asked him to come round, and when I explained he was with us in a quarter of an hour.

'Mr Harris, can you get this place safe for patients to wait in tomorrow?'

'Yes, sir' he promptly replied. 'I have looked at it and I'll have it jacked up and shored for the time being with a tarpaulin over the front and I'll get on with it early in the morning. By nine your patients will be able to come in. Will the Army be paying?' I turned to the officer, who replied: 'Yes, but I shall have to get the form for compensation and sign that and then send it up for counter signature.' I said: 'Can you tell me roughly what it says on the form?' I produced a typewriter and typed at his dictation, and then to his astonishment said, 'Mr Harris and I are going to keep you here until you sign that.' He saw two very determined locals and he signed without a murmur, had a parting drink and departed, and Mr Harris was as good as his word.

A few days later Dr Hall's nanny who used to take Philippa for a walk in the afternoons was coming back with her, holding her hand. Philippa was then five: she let go of Nanny's hand and disappeared. Nanny looked up and down the street which was completely empty at the time. Where could the child have gone? She moved on towards the front door, looking up and down the road anxiously, when the front door opened and out stepped Miss with a polite: 'Hallo Nanny, how are you?' She had picked the moment when Nanny's attention was engaged to nip under the tarpaulin, run along through the front consulting room, and out of the door.

There was a tremendous burst of activity by civilians and the Home Guard was hastily formed. Here it was taken very seriously, for we were told that invasion would almost certainly be along the flat beaches of the eastern seaboard, where landing craft could climb ashore easily: the lessons from Europe had shown that one line along the coast was useless, and that defence in depth was the best policy. The line of the Chelmer having been selected as a suitable base for pill boxes and strongpoints for the Home Guard, the Army moved in to prepare it, and local units were to liaise with them for manning, which was on a 'permanent standby' basis. Being a farming community, the manpower had to a large extent been put into the army reserve, so there was a good core of able bodied men, and the policy was to hold up any advance of invading forces for as long as possible, and then go to ground and resurface and form guerrilla groups in their rear, harassing them at night and going about our ordinary tasks by day. Many of these farm workers had done some poaching in their spare time, and were experts in undetected movement in the dark: this would have come in useful.

The doctors that remained were absorbed into First Aid posts, and men who had been physically rejected from the Home Guard itself were welcomed as stretcher bearers. Usually elderly, with varicose veins and hernias and disabilities due to rheumatism and chest diseases, they were all glad to be able to wear the uniform on an equality with their younger, fitter mates; one or two opted for what they thought was a 'soft job', but what they lacked in physical ability they made up for in enthusiasm, and attendance was good and interest was keen. We, the doctors, were expected to train them and to attend exercises and evacuate wounded: in the face of actual invasion our First Aid post was to be in the cellars of the Saracen's Head! Incidentally, my house Rood End, at the very narrowest part of the main road to Stortford, was scheduled to be demolished and pushed bodily into the road to provide one of the numerous barriers to tank movement.

The question of Daphne and the children was of course a very important one, so we planned that she should take them out to join a family of farmers at Stebbing, the Chaplins, who knew the neighbourhood well and who had a dairy herd. Mrs 'Paul' Chaplin and her two children were to join them and drive a cow up to Long Green which leads away from Bardfield to Shalford and is a remote overgrown bridleway where they thought they could hole up until the wave of invasion had passed over. So we took a suitcase with clothes out there, and we also put one at the surgery at High Easter, a small hamlet which would be unlikely to attract attention, at any rate to start with.

The signposts were all taken down and stored in depots locally: they did not return until the end of the war, so that strangers would rapidly be completely lost in the maze of small roads. I though I knew the neighbourhood pretty well by this time, but on a wet and foggy night with no lights anywhere and only the glimmer from my masked headlamps I would sometimes find myself competely adrift and have to find a house and ask where I was, which wasn't always easy. There were no white lines down the middle of roads in those days, rarely any kerbs and the verges were hazardous and sometimes had a disconcerting way of disappearing altogether.

The Fifth Column had been an upsetting feature of the European invasion, and the Government took very firm steps to try and destroy any organisation here. All enemy aliens were interned on the Isle of Man, and this of course led to great hardship but scarcely touched us: one farmer, George Lampl and his beautiful wife of Czechoslovakian Jewish extraction, had seen the inevitable spread of Nazi domination many years before, and had moved to England from his estates in Austria and had been able to bring enough cash to buy a small farm at High Roding and to set himself up there.

His very advanced methods caused a lot of head shaking in the local farming community. In those days farmers hired their combines by the week or fortnight from agricultural firms: if the harvest was not ready or it poured with rain, then it was just too bad: they had to go back to the end of the queue! Lampl bought his own combine with only two hundred acres of land, and most people thought he was mad. That harvest he hired it out to neighbours who had been let down by the regular firms because of bad weather and so on, and in two years he had paid for the combine. Most other farmers soon followed his example.

One day I was driving out towards High Roding and

passed him walking, so I stopped to ask if I could give him a lift which he gratefully accepted.

'Your car in for repairs?' I asked.

'No, they've taken it, and won't allow me even a bicycle.' I told him I was sorry.

'No — I'm glad. At last someone has seen what happened in my country, and all Europe. They've taken my telephone and my wireless; the police come out once a day to take a look at me and I feel safe!'

Air raids became much more frequent during that summer, culminating in the Battle of Britain over London in August and September. Night bombing was still a fairly rare occurrence, but the ARP was required to stand by each night as a routine. Those on duty, and for a doctor this meant every third night, were expected to sleep up at the Foakes Hall so as to be on instant call: it was difficult to sleep on the hard boards with snorers all around: each of us carried up mattresses and bedding. I solved my particular problem by commandeering the childrens' pram, and trundled my rolled-up mattress along the Stortford Road on that, but as the distance was only a couple of hundred yards I persuaded the authorities to let me sleep in bed especially as I was much more likely to be called out on ordinary night calls, and it was a great imposition for my wife or dispenser to have to dress up and come up to the Foakes Hall and get me for them.

While the Battle of Britain was at its height we took the children out to visit some friends a few miles from Dunmow with a large garden. Edmund Watts had been a junior officer in the Navy in the First World War — he was at Jutland — but in this war he was considered too elderly and too important to re-join the service, a source of considerable frustration. When we arrived his wife told us we could find him at the top of the rose garden; he had gone there to sit with an elephant gun between his knees, hoping for a stray German bomber to come low enough to have a pot shot at it. She tells me he did loose off several times in vain hope, but that he could not claim any kills.

When America entered the war they had already had some time to make preparations and almost at once they sent over their advance guard to prepare airfields. This force was the equivalent of our Pioneer Corps, really the dregs of the army: rumour had it that the jails had been opened to anyone volunteering for work overseas, and when the first arrivals appeared in Dunmow it looked as if the rumour had been justified. The poor chaps had had a long voyage across the Atlantic taking a roundabout route to lessen the risk of being torpedoed, and after weeks and weeks at sea in cramped conditions they ran a bit wild. Easton Lodge, the home of the Maynard family into whom Lady Warwick had married, was one of the first airfields to be constructed in the Eastern Counties, and a large encampment of tents had been set up for the arrival of the main force. Very few of them had ever been outside the USA, and we were a foreign nation to be treated as 'natives' in the old colonial sense. To us they seemed strange but fairly harmless: if we had expected smart soldiers in spick and span uniforms we were in for a shock, for they slouched about Dunmow in dirty khaki denims, eating whole loaves of white bread with their hands; they told us this was a great treat after their canned and frozen rations of the last six weeks. The pubs did a roaring trade, although the drinks seemed strange to them: the beer tasted funny and weak when in fact it was a good deal stronger than that to which they were accustomed. Bourbon and Rye whisky were not known, and they sniffed suspiciously at our Scotch, and an ordinary measure was regarded by them as merely a dirty glass. A double whisky was better, but it was standard practice always to order a 'double double' — four whiskies in one go: that was usually swallowed neat and in one draught when they took a long breath and settled down to the next one more slowly: their object did not seem to be the enjoyment of the drink but just to get sozzled as quickly as possible.

The trouble really started when they began mixing with the girls: they were rich, a new race with exciting new ways, and we had been asked to make them feel welcome and at home when they came over to help us. Our stodgy Victorian attitude to sex was completely foreign to their free and easy ways, and the first brushes were disastrous until both sides had come to a more mutual understanding. Quite early on a dance was organised at the Foakes Hall to welcome the Americans, and buses from neighbouring villages were arranged by the Womens Institute to bring parties of girls in as partners for our new allies. One such bus came from Felsted carrying young girls all agog in their best to meet these young men, quite innocent of their sex-starved randy intentions. The first thing they did was to take the girls off to the pub for a preliminary drink, the inevitable double double. Few of them had ever tasted whisky before, and complained that it was odd; the soldiers demanded coke to water it down, and the girls immediately swallowed it and sometimes a second, under protest.

At the end of the dance the buses waited to collect their cargo, but several girls were missing from the Felsted bus, and eventually it had to go home without them. During the next few days they turned up in very distressed and battered conditions, sometimes being unable to say where they had been: certainly some of them were taken up to the tents and kept there until they came to in horror, and being used by all and sundry until they were discovered. Several were pregnant, and one or two had venereal disease: in those days an abortion was a criminal offence, and my hands were full in dealing with broken girls and furious parents. As time went on the sexual problem settled into a regular pattern, some girls opting for the easy life and becoming genuinely fond of their American boyfriends. I talked to some of these young men, and asked why they never thought of the risks these poor girls ran and why they did not use French letters. I was solemnly assured that they were injurious to their health. A few married, and those marriages that survived seemed happy and prosperous when the couples went back to their new homes in the States. Joan, our devoted nanny, who came to our little boys very young from the Childrens Home and gave us several years of marvellous service, married a great big black American soldier. Much later she visited us with him on a trip back to England, in a huge car with the back filled with khaki picaninnies.

In due course the airfield was finished, and the proper Air Force arrived; they were splendid young men, of a very different kind. They were the cream of American youth, and welcome guests in all our houses, behaving ultra correctly and very grateful to be in an ordinary home and away from camp life. We usually had several to lunch on Sundays, they would arrive dressed in their best and surreptitiously bring small gifts for the children. These officers would shyly bring sweets and fruit, great rarities at that time: once a small sack of bananas arrived and one of

91

the children asked what they were. These were the pilots of the Barracudas who were briefed to bomb the V1 sites along the Dutch and French coasts: they would set off in formations of nine, taking off three at a time and circling until all nine were up and then away they would go. We used occasionally to watch them and once as I was going for an early morning ride to my horror I saw one explode in mid air. It was a shattering noise and for a moment all the early morning noises were silent: then there was a clamour of pheasants crowing, dogs barking, cows mooing, and birds bursting into defiant song. We used to watch for them to come home, and often there would only be four or five, the others limping home or not reappearing. When an old friend failed to turn up on a Sunday morning we refrained to ask after him for fear that he was one of the missing ones. Once on an autumn morning my old gardner was watching them take off and he remarked:

'Odd they should go out today, there'll be fog in an hour.' I replied:

'They must know what they're doing, they've got the very latest in forecasting equipment.' But he was definite and he was right. Two hours later we heard them over the dense blanket which lay over the airfield, and they landed safely at Bedford and returned to Easton late next day. I told a rather senior officer he ought to take my gardener on to the strength, and he was not amused. The war was a serious business to them, and they could not understand our joking about it: another unfortunate remark I once made was when one officer recently arrived in England turned up wearing his steel helmet, which he was loathe to part with. I told him that after the war he could always knock it flat and use it as a jerry for his infant son — stony silence. I think they had been subjected to intensive propaganda about the war, because we were having supper out at an isolated farmhouse belonging to a journalist attached to the RAF, and several USAF officers were there. The distant faint wail of the air raid warning was heard, and I turned to pass some remark to my next door neighbour to find he wasn't there. Nor were any of the other half-dozen. We finally ran them to earth in a ditch round the garden, and they were quite put out to find that we took no notice of these things.

The Americans of course brought their own doctors, who were quick to introduce themselves. I think that they were rather horrified when they discovered that at the time I was virtually single handed as my partner was unwell. Not only were they helpful in supplying items which were almost impossible to get, but on several occasions would take over my surgeries to give me a much needed rest. Quite what the patients thought, I never really discovered; but they became great friends and I was most grateful to them. After the war was over, I kept in touch with some of them, and when I started sailing again I asked one of them, Dr Morrow, if he could send me a stainless steel knife, which was impossible to buy here. He sent me one which is a treasured friend and which I still have.

Zip fasteners had only recently come into use, and I was fascinated one day when one of our officers went to the loo just before lunch, and did not reappear. We had all had a few drinks, but I did not think he could have come to any harm, so I went to look for him and asked if he needed any help. 'Yes,' he said 'this damned zip has got jammed and I can't do it up.' It was well and truly stuck, and even resisted a pair of forceps; finally I produced some safety pins and brought him back to lunch.

The American troops continued to surprise and amuse us. One summer evening Daphne and I were sitting outside the drawing room late drinking our coffee, when there was a tremendous clatter over the brick wall dividing us from the Luckins next door. A bicycle dropped apparently from heaven, followed slowly and laboriously by a dishevelled GI. He picked up the bicycle and wheeled it over to us: 'Say, is the airfield over that away?' pointing at the next garden wall. He was very drunk, I persuaded him that the easier and quicker way would be to go out into the road and then straight on towards Stortford, helped him on to his bicycle and watched him go off wobbling from side to side; I hope he got there.

The influx of evacuees brought their own problems of illness. It was before the days of the NHS, and few of them had any money or expected to pay much if at all. Their old sixpenny surgery on the corner was very different from sending me from a neighbouring village five or six miles away, and I must have clocked up a good deal of 'reward hereafter'. But it was very interesting in that it brought a different type of ailment: my year as a house surgeon in Paddington Green hospital stood me in good stead, and I had little difficulty in recognising signs and symptoms of lice, scabies and ringworm; rickets and tuberculous joints made their appearance again in quite appreciable numbers, and every sore throat was a suspected case of diphtheria until I was reasonably convinced otherwise.

I remember one case late at night in a small cottage at Broxted. It was very overcrowded with parents and three children in one small room, and my particular patient was sleeping uneasily in a half-opened bottom drawer of the chest of drawers, a small child of a year and a half with a perfectly beastly looking throat, great swollen tonsils and a yellowish horrid-looking membrane; the child was obviously toxic and ill. In those days I always carried diphtheria antitoxin with me, but the danger of giving that was one of anaphylaxis (a form of shock) as it was prepared from horse's serum, and in a sensitive child could be fatal in a few minutes. Safety lay in a tedious procedure of a test dose, a minute amount of 0.1 of a cc. given and then you had to wait for half an hour with a syringe full of adrenalin handy in case a reaction showed. Only then could you proceed to give a full dose. If it were diphtheria the antitoxin could only be a delaying process until the child got to hospital, so while I waited I had to try to persuade the parents that the only course was to remove the child to the isolation hospital: not just round the corner where they could find out how she was getting on, but well over to the other side of Chelmsford at Baddow Road, and they were most unwilling. Fortunately they had had several fatal cases in their neighbourhood so they knew the dangers of delay, but even after getting permission there was the difficulty of finding a telephone in a neighbour's house, and arranging the admission and the ambulance, trying to leave foolproof instructions for the driver to find the isolated cottage along the lanes in the dark with no signposts and only the glimmer from his masked headlights. I suppose he arrived a couple of hours later, but it seemed to be all night, and the stuffy crowded room and the crying children, both parents in tears, and above all the ill child, left one of those impressions that lasts.

There was a brief epidemic of gastro-enteritis amongst the babies, which did not stop until one or two died from it: sadly there was little to do for them and this was one of the facts of life in those days.

One whole nursery was evacuated down to Newton Hall, and a local girl who was a trained childrens' nurse volunteered to take charge of the twenty-odd children. She was a great success, became a close personal friend and married one of the masters at Felsted; at one time she took on the school sanatorium and was equally successful there until she started her own family. But the nursery was great fun, and I thoroughly enjoyed my visits there, mostly routine, but occasionally a serious case. One of these was fatal rapidly, rather too old to be a cot death, but along those lines. Few of the children had been immunised against diphtheria, and it was one of the first things I organised. I had noticed that on a hot night the children threw their bedclothes off them and often ended up sleeping in a curled up kneeling position with their little bare bottoms sticking out invitingly, so I told Sister I would come along after supper with my needles, and I proceeded to walk down the row of little behinds giving a jab to each one and they hardly seemed to notice beyond a stir and a wriggle and making themselves more comfortable. At Christmas time I was invited to be Father Christmas, so I dressed up in gumboots and a red dressing gown with a beard of cotton wool, and I was smuggled in up the stairs while the children were gathered in the hall at the foot waiting the arrival of the Great Man. When I did step down the effect was most unexpected; there was a universal howl of terror, a wild stampede, and in two seconds the hall was empty and the children had disappeared.

Off with the dressing gown and gumboots, on with my ordinary jacket, I re-entered the usual way by the front door and all was well again.

My partner had gone to the war, and a neighbouring doctor at Hatfield Broad Oak had disappeared — he was reputed to have taken a boat to New Zealand as a ship's doctor; he just walked out and left nobody to take his place. Dr Hall was old and sympathetic, but very asthmatic, he had been through the first war and was valiantly carrying on but as soon as he could after the war he retired and in fact died quite soon after that: my friend Dr Roberts who was his junior partner and had come at about the same time as myself, was also in poor health and overworked; the local war medical committee occasionally sent me a locum, but they were a poor lot — the first was a charming retired orthopaedic surgeon who had no clue. He tried hard for a week and was almost in tears when he told me that it was too much for him, but in fact it was a relief because he was no good and it took up more time telling him what to do than to get on with it myself. I had two fairly advanced drug addicts, and one splendid character who was with me for some time and was in fact a marvellous GP — when he was sober. He was a very large man and strikingly handsome in his way, and well-turned out in a navy blue suit with a row of First World War medals peeping out from under his lapel. He had a limp and some weakness in his right arm, due to having been blown up by a mine. He told me he was teetotal, and I think he honestly may have been at the time; he started at Felsted and was a great success at the beginning, although he had a tendency to treat the locals as 'natives', explaining that he had practised abroad for a number of years.

It was some time before I began to hear disconcerting rumours, and even to receive complaints. At first it was simply that he was rather too thorough in his examination of the prettier girls, and a malicious tale-bearer said that no matter what complaint a girl had, he would yell at her 'Strip'! It was quite evident that he was not teetotal because one night he just disappeared, and there was nobody in the surgery or at his digs for the next three days. Then I was telephoned in the evening by the landlord of the local, asking me to come and take him away as he had dug himself in there and had refused to move for the last three days.

He went, and the war committee sent me a substitute, a woman, and a very efficient doctor, particularly in obstetrics. Unfortunately she was a red-hot Socialist, if not a Communist. An old friend who lived in a large house with three children all away at school rang me up and complained that she had paid no attention to her symptoms, but had simply said 'Do you mean to say that you live alone in this great big house? It could easily house three or four poor families that I know of.' Apart from this tendency, however, she worked well and loyally and saw me out until the end of the war.

Meanwhile I was working very long hours, the Home Guard was taking up quite a lot of time in the evenings, and I found the only thing to do was to start early in the morning visiting for perhaps an hour before a break for breakfast then the surgery in Dunmow followed by one at Felsted. Any necessary visits there, and then back to Dunmow where I picked up a driver, one of the small devoted band of ladies who took on the job of helping me as part of their war work. She would drive me out to Hatfield Broad Oak to a surgery there, with visits on the way: and she might have her sandwich and a coffee while I was doing the surgery, and I would eat mine as we drove out to more visits in that neighbourhood; and then back to Dunmow to pick up messages and on two days a week out to the Rodings and High Easter with surgeries and visits there. Back again in the evenings to the surgery in Dunmow once more, with possibly more visits that had come in from Felsted, the Eastons or Stebbing, but these were mostly the territory of the 'other firm'. Sometimes in desperation I would ask them to see one or two of my cases which I knew they would be passing, but neither the patients nor they liked it much: it was a very close association between doctor and patient in those days, which could have considerable disadvantages at times. This same life went on day after day, week after week and year after year, with no break at all. One summer in desperation I took to sleeping in a caravan out at Tilty; it was a respite. Poor Daphne would answer the telephone and tell them that I was out, I could not be got hold of, and she had no idea when I would be back, it was no good ringing again, and if they were sufficiently worried they must get another doctor. Those nights were pure bliss; I slept peacefully on a camp bed practically out in the open, and woke in the morning to cattle poking inquisitive noses in at the door, and the sound of birds singing and pheasants crowing: a covey of partridges would pass between the caravan and the hedge every morning at about the same time, led by the cock and the chicks rather like a school crocodile; little clumps of two or three, chattering away and diving off to investigate something interesting or pick up a grub, to be chased back by mum who followed up in the rear. I looked forward to their visit, and was worried if I had to leave before they put in an appearance.

The only other break I remember was when I went to Brighton for five days to recover from an attack of hepatitis, infectious jaundice, although we were only just beginning to realise that it was an infection. Dr Pickles

97

classic account of the spread of this disease in his Yorkshire dale had not come my way though it was published just before the war, in 1938. The evidence was being collected from outbreaks which had occurred in isolated communities such as troop carriers at sea for a long time and besieged towns. Anyway I had got more and more irritable and depressed until the children were saying 'What's wrong with Daddy?'. At that point Daphne asked Francis Camps to have a look at me, and he packed me off to bed until the jaundice had subsided sufficiently for me to appear in public when I went to Brighton.

I also was able to get away on another occasion due to the kindness of R. A. Butler, then Minister of Education, who was a Governor of Felsted School which had been evacuated to Herefordshire. As I was still the official Medical Officer to the school, he insisted that I accompanied him to see how they were faring in their temporary home. I can well remember the luxury of the first class carriage as I slept while he did his 'boxes' and then in typical fashion, as there were spare seats in the compartment, he invited some soldiers who were standing in the corridor to take them. I had a few days fishing with the doctor who had taken over from me at Leominster, and was also able to see my son who was at the Junior House at Canon Ffrome, where I again fished with the local carpenter. I was able to repeat this visit again towards the end of the war, when the new headmaster, Alistair Andrews, invited me down to discuss the move back to Essex.

During the war a number of German aeroplanes were shot down in Essex, and sometimes their occupants baled out and landed safely. Early one summer morning the police rang me up to say that there were two wounded Germans at Poplars Farm, but when I asked which Poplars Farm they told me they had no other information. I set off and visited five different ones in succession, taking the points of the compass in turn starting with the north and going to the east and then to the south and in each case a matter of six or seven miles. When I finally went west, I found them.

It was a farm which was run by two elderly spinsters after the death of their father, who had been a splendid character with a great big Old Testament beard and a remarkably gentle and benevolent nature. I knocked on their door and asked them whether they knew of any German parachutists in the neighbourhood, and the elder one said,

'Do come in, doctor, and see for yourself.' She showed me into their kitchen where two rather frightened big blond boys in uniform looked up from a lavish breakfast of bacon and eggs. The sisters explained that the soldiers knew just a little English, enough to answer their questions as to whether they were hungry and if they would like some breakfast. They appeared so frightened and lost that the two old ladies felt the only thing to do was to give them a good meal which they would be able to remember during the long imprisonment they obviously would face over here.

Another parachutist came down half way between Dunmow and Braintree. It was in the early morning, and I suppose he had heard of our Home Guard, because he was petrified and determined to give himself up to the first person he could find rather than to fall into the hands of these blood-thirsty patriots. He came down the road and walked along it until he reached the first house which was the Saling Oak Inn, whose landlady was a well known character, especially in her methods of dealing with uproarious American airmen from the nearby base. The parachutist banged on the door and the sleepy landlady put her head out of the window. Seeing a uniform below she assumed that it was a thirsty US airman. She told him in no uncertain terms what he could do with himself, but the man looked up at her and said in halting English,

'I am a German airman.'

Whereupon the lady replied, 'Well, I'm Mae West, come up and see me some time,' slammed the window down and went back to bed.

A few land mines were also dumped over Essex, always in fields, where they made enormous holes and occasionally killed a heifer. Some did not explode, and these were treated at first with great respect, but when nothing happened until the bomb disposal squad arrived to take away the huge piece of metal with its beautifully attached nylon cord and vast parachute, the bolder spirits would go in first and cut away the loot. One of these unexploded landmines was in a field belonging to a Scottish lady who lived at Barnston who was the first to arrive on the scene and with no hesitation she walked up and cut away the ropes and parachute which she bundled into the back of her Daimler and took home. She was a patient and a good friend, and I still have lengths of the beautiful parachute cord on the staircase of my cottage in Devon; the stairs are very steep and circular and as I swing myself easily up or down I think gratefully of the givers, Scot or German.

One aeroplane crashed in flames just outside Dunmow, and at first there was great rejoicing because we thought it was a German raider. The joy turned to sadness when it was discovered that this was one of the victims of the habit of German nightfighters to follow a British plane home until it was near its base when the tail gunner was liable to relax, and the Germans would come in for a quick kill from below and behind.

People who lived in the country were encouraged by the Government to be as self-supporting as possible, and to grow more food. This applied not only to vegetables and fruit, poultry and eggs, but also to starting pigs and bees, and we did both. Each pig had to be shared by two people, who would keep another pig for the Government; so I went into partnership with my gardener, and we purchased two little pigs who I think were two months old, with the understanding that they would go to the bacon factory at six months. One would then go for the nation, and the other would be divided between us. We were allowed to buy rations for the pigs, and the Government paid a certain amount towards the keep and purchase of their pig. When the pigs arrived there was great interest in the family, especially from my two children and I think I promptly christened them Nicolas and Philippa after them, so inevitably when the next pair arrived they were named after their father and mother! We became quite fond of them, and found that they were animals of great character, capable of returning affection, although how much of it was cupboard love associated with food is anyone's guess. They appreciated being scratched, and this the children would do happily, and I was surprised to find what clean animals they were in their straw. Philippa was heart-broken when they finally went to the factory, and she could not be persuaded to eat any of the delicious bacon that came back. The hams I used to take at first to a patient who was an expert, out at the village shop at Keers Green; she would smoke them herself. After a while I grew more ambitious and learnt how to cure them myself, with black treacle and nitre. Then I used to take them to be smoked at the factory — it was a very family affair in those days. It was known as the Dunmow Flitch Bacon Factory, and the proprietor and many of the people who worked there were personally known to me as patients. Our pigs used to go out to Keers Green to be killed, and I would come back next day with a tin bath full of the oddments which we converted rather messily into brawn and we had a great feast of liver and so on. I suppose we must have had half a dozen series of pigs in our time.

The bees at first were a great success. I bought two hives, and was given the swarms; I was taught by an old beekeeper who had been a horseman to one of my patients. He provided me with a veil and bellows, but he never wore anything himself, and handled the bees gently and expertly, occasionally brushing one off his neck if it got too friendly. The Government allowed us to buy a ration of sugar for them, which he advised me was more than they needed: so my children benefited by the extra ration, and the great moment arrived at the end of the summer when we took the honey, which was a great success — everyone helped, and the children were in a permanent state of sickness for several days.

All went well until one of my hives swarmed, and a patient kindly offered me one of his spare swarms. Now these were Italian bees, and I am not sure whether they took after their race or their donor, for they were fiery, fierce and unpredictable, and one day they decided to set about me in no mean fashion. I had a fair number of stings and was quite ill as a result: but I went back to them, well protected as I thought, until constant stings began to produce alarming reactions, and I had to give the hive away. The following winter saw the end, because I was so busy in the practice that I did not look after them well: when I came to open them up in the spring I found nothing. The dreaded moth had got in and destroyed the hibernating bees, so I gave the hives to my friend the beekeeper, and from then on he used to keep me supplied with plenty of his own delicious combs. I suppose I was spoilt, but I never did appreciate run-honey and always preferred to eat it straight in the comb.

Amusements and holidays were very rare and limited in a small country town, but we did our best for the children; in summertime we joined with friends for picnics, either down by the river where on a fine warm day they would bathe in a wider stretch about two miles downstream from Dunmow, then have a great game of hide-and-seek or whatever it was, in which we grownups used to join. There was still a cinema in Dunmow, the 'flea pit', where the sound from the film was often drowned by the noisy flushing of the cistern in the loo just by the entrance. The films that came down were out of date but extremely good and many were suitable for the children and again great parties were made up. We were always made to go well in time so as to be able to choose our seats.

The authorities were very good to these small scattered communities and made it easy for circuses and occasional fairs to tour the neighbourhood. The field by the church was where the tents were put up, and there used to be enormous excitement among the children who would hang around watching preparations and get in early in the queue when the fair or circus opened. The latter were very simple affairs, but enjoyed just as much; the atmosphere was intimate so that the clowns were able to establish a rapport quickly and the children all collapsed with laughter at very simple jokes. One of the highlights was when the ringmaster asked for any small volunteers to come and ride on the 'liberty horse', a huge grey who solemnly went round and round while the girls on her back danced and performed acrobatics and finally dived through a paper hoop. The ringmaster explained that the way he trained young circus riders was by fitting them into a harness on the end of a long arm which rotated on the central pole, so that they could not fall off and were perfectly safe. He would install a small boy on the horse's back in the harness, then give the signal and Dobbin would first walk and then trot with the master pushing the bar round in time with the horse. When this had gone on for a little time and the child was beginning to grow confident and perhaps dance a step or two, he would quietly encourage the horse to go that little bit faster, and while encouraging the small boy to run to keep up he would gently slow the bar so that finally the boy was left in mid-air, running hard to catch the horse which had gone on ahead, and this really brought the house down.

At the end of the war there had to be a 'Victory Parade' which was made up of the Home Guard, Air Raid Wardens, WVS, Fire Service and all the organisations which had been part of Dunmow's war effort. I was told that I would have to appear, and was not very keen. However I reached agreement finally with the local Home Guard commander who gave me permission (as I was then a Lieutenant-Colonel) to ride a horse, so Paddy was pressed into military service and to my surprise behaved very well. Perhaps he realised that hunting might begin again.

CHAPTER VIII

TIME OFF

Why does a doctor choose to live in the country? He must give up ambition to become either famous or wealthy, he must be prepared to spend his life as an ordinary general practitioner, and — at any rate when I started to work — be on call for twenty four hours a day 365 days a year except when he was on holiday. Fifty years ago hospitals regarded us as having 'slipped off the ladder of the specialist' in the words of our Dean, who became Lord Moran. In fact he did not mean it in quite such a deprecating sense, because I remember his coming down to see a case of mine and sitting in my very pleasant consulting room on a summer evening with the windows wide open looking out into the walled Georgian garden and musing to himself:

'I wonder, if I had it all over again and knew that it was like this whether I wouldn't have chosen it.'

What did you get in exchange? I think I chose it largely by accident, but I soon realised that if I stayed on in the locum I was doing I should be free of the rush and competition, the rat race of the London consultants competing for paying cases. There was a pleasant house to live in, an adequate income for country needs, and a good base for a wife and family. Although my home had never been in the country, having been brought up first in India and then on the edge of Cambridge, I had always longed to be a countryman and here was the chance. The patients were the farmers, farm workers and people connected with the farming industry, and with no disrespect to town folk, more likeable, less demanding and self-reliant.

Besides giving up ambition, financial and professional, it also meant doing without many of the recreations which I had grown fond of, such as the theatre and the cinema, concerts and picture exhibitions, in fact the cultural life of a city: on the other hand this new life offered opportunities of learning exciting new things about horses, guns and dogs.

My father had spent a great deal of his life in the very primitive countryside of Southern India as a botanist and agricultural adviser. He had used a horse as a means of transport as well as enjoying it, and I don't think he regularly went for a ride for the sheer pleasure. He shot game a good deal, but for the pot. Again, he enjoyed the sport, but he was quite prepared to take an easy shot rather than risk a difficult one if it would mean something for supper. When he came home he had sold his gun, and certainly never went near a horse again. He had never tried to fish or to sail, so I had not had encouragement along those lines. His recreations were tennis and gardening and poultry, and I had had several years working in the orchard and playing tennis with him. (His tennis was of a deadly nature — he stood quite still and placed his returns alternately to each side of the court ending up with a powerful 'cut shot' which was very fashionable in Victorian days, and which suddenly lay down and refused to rise from the bounce as you ran for it.)

So I was completely green, but here was a marvellous opportunity and as I got to know a few of the farmers and patients, I found everyone only too anxious to help and teach a beginner. Shooting and riding were on one's doorstep, and well within my pocket if I was not too ambitious. And patients understood so well if you were not there all the time, but were out doing something they themselves understood rather than off to London which was much farther and more mysterious (and wicked, to the country people who had largely never been there themselves). As time went on and my tastes got known, it was touching how much people would do to help. On a Saturday morning if I were doing the surgery wearing a stock, breeches and boots, the first patient in was quite liable to say:

'Oh doctor, I didn't realise you were going hunting — I can do another day,' walk straight out, and when I went into the waiting room to get the next patient I might find that the rest had followed in a body!

I remember, too, taking my gun in the back of the car with gumboots and my dog, thinking that I should get half-an-hour to spare to walk one or two hedges at Brands Farm. There was a tractor working a couple of fields away, and I noticed the driver stop and get out, and walk across the plough towards me. I thought 'Oh bother, I suppose he wants me to go in and see one of his family,' but not a bit of it. He said,

'Doctor, it's no good your walking down that hedge; a

105

couple of boys went along that half-an-hour ago and they put all the birds into that little spinney; you go straight there.' And he trudged back across the plough.

So I have tried to remember those early days of hunting and shooting and tell it in gratitude to all who have helped me, and perhaps to encourage others who start late but can still enjoy this type of 'Time off' as much as I have.

HUNTING

When I started in practice in Dunmow I was far too busy in my first few years, to think of riding, which I had only done rather half-heartedly as a child in India, but after five years I looked round and decided that I could now make a start, so I went to Captain Palmer who ran a riding school at Bishops Stortford. He was a splendid fellow, and only said: 'I suppose you want to be given a refresher course?' I told him I had to start absolutely at the beginning with no previous experience, and he took me on those terms. After a few months he suggested a quiet day's hunting with him on one of his schoolmaster horses, with the Puckeridge. The great day arrived and I kept close to Captain Palmer and tried not to show how excited I was at the age of thirty for my first day's hunting. I went several times after that; I knew the old Master through visits to mutual friends at Quendon Hall. He was a splendid old man, and very friendly to me: he used to come out on a wise old cob, and always dressed in a covert coat of dark brown with huge pearl buttons and a brown bowler. I would ride alongside him and he would say:

'Go on young man, don't wait for me, you've got a fine horse there' (Captain Palmer's old grey), 'off you go and don't hang about.' And off I went, only to find at the first check that the old man would be there long before me. When this happened several times I asked him how he did it and he replied, 'Bless you, I know the names of all these foxes and where they'll make for; I just slip along and watch him and wait for you all to catch up.' I replied: 'I suppose you know where he's gone now?' And he gave me a nice smile and said, 'Maybe, but I won't spoil it.'

A year later I stayed in Surrey and went with my brother-in-law with the Old Surrey and Burstow and was duly blooded. He put me on a good safe horse and told me only to jump what he jumped first, I got a bit behind and the chap in front of me knocked his hat off on an overhanging bough just as I was taking off. To my horror I looked straight down my horse's foreleg into the crown of his beautiful top hat and we went away wearing a neat stocking with a very angry gentleman in pursuit.

'Being blooded' reminds me of years later when I took a small girl from London on Philippa's pony, very keen, and we had the luck to kill a fox and she also was blooded. Tradition prevented her from washing her face before she went off in the train to London that evening, and she told me that an old lady in the carriage said, 'Little girl, your face is very dirty — it looks like blood on it.'

'Yes,' replied the child, and proudly prattled of the details to the horrified looks of the entire carriage, finally opening her suitcase and proudly displaying the gory mask that she was taking home to be mounted.

But all that was after the War when I had started hunting regularly on a horse of my own. Up to the war I depended on other people who were very generous. The Gibsons at Battailes had a string, and I used to exercise with George and any of the children who were about. It was when Lady Warwick was still alive in the Lodge, and she was very kind in allowing us to ride in the park: years before there were beautiful made-up gallops, the three furlong and the five furlong: now they were very rough, and riddled with rabbit holes. It didn't prevent our racing, and George always used to hang behind cheering us on. Fifty yards from the end he would go into top gear, make a splendid race of it, and win by a short head. But occasionally we took an almighty fall. I had an assistant, Dr Rees, young, totally inexperienced, and enormously enthusiastic. He was game for anything, and one day he came a phenomenal purler. I caught his horse at the park gate, bound his head up, and put him up to take him back to the surgery to stitch it: an awkward star-shaped cut which took some time and he made no murmur. Years later an old lady talking of her previous illness said: 'That was when I was so ill and you had that young Dr Rees.' I looked at her record and saw some trifling entry, and said, 'What made you think you were so ill then?' 'It was that young Dr Rees, the assistant; he'd come off his horse and was wearing a great bandage: he must have seen me six times that evening, and we all got so worried.' I had told him to go to bed as he was concussed, but he insisted on finishing his round, and obviously hadn't a clue what he was doing.

The war came, my younger partner went, and I was left on my own. One of Daphne's cousins had a beautiful thoroughbred hunter which she offered me if I could take it just to keep it fed, as she could get no hay. With the days of the invasion scare, running three practices, Home Guard and all that, there was no question, but when things did settle down and it was obvious that we were going to have a long spell of hard work and no holiday I cleared out the empty loose box at Rood End, took in a supernumerary horse of Edwin Baker's, and got in an early morning ride most days to keep me sane. His name was Paddy and he was a grand type of Irish horse. He existed on straw and very occasional hay, sweepings from barn floors, and potato peelings, as well as any of the outsides of cabbages and apple cores that Philippa could scrape together, and lawn-mowings, which were strictly forbidden by all the pundits but never seemed to do him much harm. Philippa adored him. He stood 16.2 and to groom him she had to stand on a soap box. The conversation used to be very interesting when she didn't think I was listening, he was told all the news, was given intimate glimpses into her eight-year-old private life, and when he gave an appreciative swish of his tail and knocked her off her box he was told in very plain terms exactly what she thought of his behaviour. (Where do they pick these words up?)

Later on I heard some remarkable language from a small girl out hunting. It was a great big ditch in the Rodings, and just her head poking out as she moved along on her pony at the bottom of the ditch:

'You so and so idiot of a horse, you got me in here and you've got to so and so get me out again!'

There is a saying that you own the little bit of land that you land on when you come off a horse; if so, I have quite a nice little property scattered all round this part of the world. When I started hunting after the war the Roding ditches upset many much better horsemen than I was. I remember once coming down on the landing side and immediately afterwards Freeman Robinson doing the same thing beside me. He didn't turn a hair, but merely turned to me on the ground and remarked:

'Imitation is the sincerest form of flattery, Geoffrey.'

After the war ended, I bought a little four-year-old cob mare called Cockayne, very willing, very green like me, and we set out to learn together. To start with she couldn't jump at all, preferring to blunder her way through obstacles, which was very popular with the fainter-hearted members of the field: 'Wait for the doctor, he'll knock it down.' But in time she found that rails ought to be respected, and developed a reasonable jump. But she was unpredictable and would sometimes give the most enormous leap from a standstill and would jump me off, or at best I would land round her neck.

She gave me four good years, and then I got tired of being permanently left behind with even the small children dashing by, spooning up the mud in my face, and decided to buy something a little bit faster; so I bought a very nice looking big grey called Smokey Joe. He was stabled at Much Hadham, so I thought it would be quite a reasonable ride to hack back here if I took it in leisurely fashion. I had got no further than Stortford when he began to get slower and slower. I had tried him a couple of days before and he seemed to go well then, so I was puzzled but there was nothing to do but persevere and I ended up walking the last two miles with him into Dunmow, as he obviously simply couldn't go on carrying me. I rang up the chap I had bought him off who was mystified, but he suggested that I waited a few days before sending him back: two days later the poor horse developed a sharp attack of jaundice. After about three weeks he seemed to have recovered completely, but he never really went well after that; he would run for perhaps twenty minutes or half an hour and then suddenly 'blow up'. He would drop to a slow walk and have to recover his wind before going on. He was a very handsome horse and looked a treat, with perfect manners; so I had no difficulty in selling him to a man who wanted him for film work!

A word about expense. When I bought Cockayne she cost me £45. I bought a secondhand hunting coat for £5, very well cut, from a tailor in Winchester, before the war; my boots were by Maxwell's, given me by an old patient who had no further use for them; my spurs, whip and breeches came from my brother-in-law and his father. I wore a city bowler to start with, so the only outlay in kit

109

was a pair of riding gloves and a stock. Old Stock the smith, used to charge £1 for putting on a set of new shoes, with an extra 5/- for a new set of Mordax studs when I had them fitted after slipping up on an icy road. They were made with a hard steel centre and a softer case all round, so that as they wore down they were always sharp, and as they screwed into the shoes they were used time and again and one set lasted the whole season.

Philippa started riding at the same time as I did, and the Gibsons handed over Mouse, their old schoolmaster pony, a dear little horse which he had bought off Frinton sands and which had taught all their family to ride. When Philippa grew out of it she passed it on to another family to teach them and I think Mouse went into retirement when four of them had all learnt on her back. As Philippa grew she had a series of ponies, and we rode early in the morning most of the year until she left her day school at sixteen. We had to go early so that she could get back in time to change and have her breakfast and catch the bus into Bishop's Stortford which she did in record time; I took her horse at the gate, and by the time I had fed them and turned them out she was waiting at the bus stop.

In the autumn I usually took a haversack with me to stock up with mushrooms which grew in profusion in those days on the grassy meadows towards Little Dunmow. The dogs used to come with us, including Tara the springer spaniel who insisted on following when she was quite a tiny puppy. At the bottom of Bumpstead Hill there was a stream which sometimes flooded, and half way through I suddenly thought of the little puppy, much too deep for her. I looked round and there she was, gamely swimming. Riding up through Cobb's Wood one morning we disturbed a badger and two cubs who ran squeaking for home: a lovely sight. Better still, on a snowy winter's morning just as the sun was rising, to watch a flight of eleven herons crossing the red rising sun over the river like a picture on a Japanese screen. We often set out in pitch darkness in winter and watched the sun rise, sometimes there was still a moon, and I remember once remarking to Philippa that it really was a 'blue moon'.

It was great fun when Philippa got sufficiently handy to be able to come hunting with me. We hacked to all the meets, and sometimes a friend of hers would take my horse on, going leisurely with Philippa chattering the whole way, so that I could go later to the meet by car. One-and-a-half to two hours to hack to the further meets in the Saturday country, High Easter, Good Easter and so on, and coming home I would tap on the window from my horse at Mrs Roger's stores in High Roding and out she would bring orangeade for Philippa and a bucket of water for her pony. My horse tended to turn automatically into the yard of one of the pubs where I had beer brought out in the same way.

One of our early expeditions was when we went cubbing together in September. We had been running a fox and I was called back because someone had come down in a muddy lane and was in rather a mess. I found a small girl with her face covered in mud and blood. A stream ran down the sides of the lane so I dipped my handkerchief in that and started to clean her up. I suppose I was making soothing noises, 'how did it happen?' and so on, when I was astonished to hear her addressing me as 'Papa'. Poor Philippa! She was always plucky, and came home quite cheerfully but we spent some time at the horse trough in the stables at the park before daring to walk the half mile home to face her mother.

I replaced Smokey Joe with Uncle Tom. He was quite a different horse, standing at 16.3, strong, heavily built and reasonably fast, and would go on all day. He was very keen, and could jump anything, easy to catch and shoe, and those were his good points.

But there is always the other side of the penny, and first there was his appearance. He was a coloured horse: a proper gipsy skewbald, brown and white, common-looking and ugly, and very conspicuous especially if his saddle was empty! He hated passing a stationary car and would make a wide sweep around it, which didn't usually matter except when it happened in the crowded High Street of Dunmow with cars parked on either side. I spent hours trying to cure him of the habit, and it was quite hopeless. He came to me beautifully clipped out, but it was the last time he looked like that, for he had a rooted objection to having his head clipped. The first time I put a twitch on him he lifted me, twitch and all, up to the roof of the stable: after that I used to take him to the vet in Braintree, and even he had difficulty. Once he overdid his injection of tranquilliser, and he had not come round properly when

I started back through the town.

But he gave me some marvellous hunts. There was one from Chignall Smealey, when the fox ran as usual to the drain at Broomfield in the grounds of the hospital just outside Chelmsford. But he couldn't quite make it, and turned into a garden, and disappeared into thin air. Hounds were clamouring at the gate of the walled kitchen garden, so Watchorn the huntsman got off his horse and let them in, with the field outside watching over the wall. They made straight for the door of the garden shed in the corner, and when the huntsman opened it they shot in and out popped the fox from the chimney. He landed on the garden path amongst all the horses, and wriggled out towards the rose garden, but there the pack got him, and the owner of the garden, who was out with the hunt, had his brush as a treasured trophy.

Those were wonderful hunting days, with a number of very active old men who remembered the early 1900s. I delighted in talking to them and drawing out their reminiscences. Once we were in a field near Aythorpe Roding from which we could see the spires of the churches of High Easter and White Roding. Tom Howard and Llewellyn Marriage were by me and I heard one of them say to the other: 'Wasn't this where we started for an early point-to-point?' I asked about it and was told that all they had to do was to make their own way round each church where someone was stationed to tick them off his list, and the first back in the field would win. I saw a photograph of the start in one of the cottages, and like a fool did not ask for it when the patient died.

Uncle Tom gave me four or five very good seasons, and then I had a marvellous stroke of luck. Bill Hutley offered me his point-to-point horse Beeswork, who had won a number of point-to-points as a young horse, gone lame and been rested and fired, tried again but done no good. Bill had bought a younger horse and had no room for Beeswork who was only fourteen and perfectly capable of giving a good day's hunting. Would I like him? He warned that he was a strong horse with a will of his own, but he was an absolute dream to look at and most aristocratically bred. On his sire's side there was the great Gainsborough Sansovino, and further back St Simon: on his dam's side Tetratema, Phalaris, and The Tetrarch, and he looked all of it. In a dozen point-to-points he had been first in five of them and placed in all the rest.

I had some fairly hairy rides on him to start with, until I got the measure of him. He had two speeds, flat out and stop (when you could). I was warned to try no bit except a snaffle, and I managed to hold him although it was wise to use two reins. At first I got George, the retired groom of Mr Watts, to exercise him for me when he came up from grass, and early on Beeswork broke a rein and had a fine career across half Essex before George could stop him. His one idea was racing.

But he was absolutely marvellous in every other way. The easiest horse in the stable — kind, never kicked, friendly and inquisitive — he leaned his head over your shoulder and looked to see what you were doing, and grandchildren could run about under him and sit on his back and slide off into the straw and he merely looked round with interest. Traffic was no trouble; what a change from Uncle Tom! We used to go to be shod in Stock's yard off Dunmow High Street, and the traffic could be roaring in all directions without his turning a hair and he stopped automatically at the Belisha beacon. Boxing was no problem at all — you merely put the tailboard down and he shot up the ramp. He was very indignant when another horse was put into the box and he was shut out.

It was out hunting that my troubles began, because he would not stand: I learnt early on that if you put him on grass you had to let him go otherwise he would nap and buck until he had me off. Once I had hacked him the whole way to Woodside Green, eight or nine miles, and he was so fresh at the meet that I took him into a ploughed field and put him round it three or four times to try to cool him off, but not a bit of it; it only freshened him up, and coming out he tried to jump over the bonnet of a car. The first meet I went to, a lady came up and said,

'What a beautiful horse, Geoffrey; where did you get him from?' I told her and she said, 'God, take him away — I got on him once for a lady's point-to-point and just managed to get him down to the start, then he went off like a rocket, shot over the first fence, and put me in hospital for ten days.'

He was a marvellous horse in the way that he would go off alone; horses don't usually like it, and they get bored and sluggish. Not him; he always gave a me a gay ride and I had eleven years of bliss.

Much of the country in Essex is ploughed fields, so that hunting is very different from the grass lands of the shires, and consequently looked on by many as an inferior form of sport. This entirely depends on the attitude of the rider, whether he wants a tremendous gallop over grass with lots of good fences to jump, hounds running long and straight and hard, often away in the distance; or whether he wants to watch the pack working, puzzling out a line over the cold plough, catching a whiff here and running on until the scent fades and they have to cast round to find where it lingers once again, gently encouraged at times by the huntsman, but more often left to work it out themselves as a wise pack will. They run slower because of the difficulty of the land and because of their breeding, being bred for 'nose' rather than 'pace'. E. S. Bovill, writing in his book *The England of Nimrod and Surtees* tells of the great Mr Assheton-Smith over a hundred years ago who gave up the Mastership of the Quorn to return to his native Hampshire for this very reason: namely that he preferred to devote his life to houndwork rather than to the hurry and the skelter of the fashionable shires. Our huntsman was watching the pack worrying out a line in a scrubby old overgrown green lane, when a bright young spark came by and remarked, 'Goodness, Tom, I can smell fox all right here.'

A few minutes later a girl came up and made almost the same remark. Tom turned away and muttered, 'We'd better breed from those two for next season.'

A word about grooms. Mine were all very part-time, being pressed into service from the garden: all of them had had experience of horses, being brought up with them like any countryman at that time: not all of them would admit to it and one or two were distinctly nervous at first. First of all was Whybrow, the gardener that we inherited when we took Dr Tench's house. He had started as a groom for Tench when he went round in a horse and trap, and later became his chauffeur when he took to a motor car. He was an old man then, and in fact hardly lasted long enough to look after a horse of mine. I chiefly remember him for being very kind to the children when they were small. He was addicted to a perfectly foul old pipe; and he was once observed to quieten Nicolas, who had tipped up his pram and had fallen out, by taking the pipe out of his own mouth and sticking it into the baby's, who apparently sucked quite contentedly and was then stunned into tranquillity. He was replaced by Ardley, a splendid little man, who had started as a handyman in one of the Dunmow pubs, and had to look after horses as they came into the yard. From there he moved to cleaning buses, and thankfully came to us as a gardener-handyman. He got on well with the horses, but nothing would induce him to mount one. He was completely tireless and used to boast that in the First World War he marched as an infantryman the whole way to Berlin and the whole way back. When I was sawing wood with him, although he was about half my size, he worked at a steady rate and could go on for hours long after I was gasping. As a child he used to tell us that he was one of eight and brought up on his father's agricultural wage of twelve shillings a week. One of the great events of the year was the annual visit to the Chelmsford Agricultural Show in August. The whole family used to prepare a basket of food and they would set off at five in the morning to walk the twelve miles each way, including the tiddlers who would have to be carried along with the food at intervals. The journey took about four hours, and they kept going with songs and simple games. At the end of the long, hot day there would be the journey home, pretty well walking in their sleep and having to be picked up and carried from time to time. Next day work as usual for the older ones, but it provided a subject of conversation for weeks afterwards.

I have said that Ardley was a spare wiry little man. His wife by contrast was huge. She really was enormous and you looked twice at her. One year we took them both to the Essex Show which was being held in Saffron Walden. We went to the turnstiles, and the young attendant took one look at Mrs Ardley and politely opened the little gate and said,

'Try this way, Missus.'

'None of your lip, young man,' she replied, and edged into the turnstile and stuck absolutely fast there. The more she wriggled the tighter she stuck; people started laughing and Mrs Ardley became furious, first of all with her poor husband, 'Take that silly grin off your face, you'll catch it when I get out of here,' as he faded still chuckling into the

115

crowd. The folk who went in did not spare their wit, and poor Mrs Ardley alternately glowered and swore at them until the attendant returned with a mechanic who solemnly unscrewed the top of the barrier and released her to go in search of her husband. We did not see them until we left, and they were a very silent pair going home.

A day out hunting brings many pleasures apart from the actual sport; the chance to see the countryside at leisure, Thaxted in the distance with its church and windmill standing up boldly over the bare ploughland; the lovely Ashdon woods in early spring with tips of green and pussy willow showing everywhere, and a chorus of bird song. A stubble field out near Tilty which was swarming with pheasants, and the master telling the field to spread out and go slowly because he felt sure there was a fox amongst them. Sure enough, there was, but he must have been sound asleep with a couple of pheasants inside him, for he had no chance to run more than a few yards before he was 'chopped' by the eager pack.

I remember an early spring at the end of the season, waiting in a ride in the shelter of a wood in the sunshine, drowsing and listening to Tom encouraging hounds at the far end of the wood. Basking in the warm sunshine was an old point-to-pointer (Beeswork's contemporary) with his head drooping and his eyes shut. 'Heather, I think your horse is fast asleep.' She fished in her pocket and produced a ginger biscuit. 'Hold that under his nose.' 'Dead,' I said, after a minute. Then slowly, his nostrils twitched, his eyes opened; up went his head and down went the biscuit.

Finally there was the pleasure of coming home, companionship and gossip either jogging along or back in the horsebox: that first cigarette or cigar (before I had to give up smoking), the final draining of a whisky flask or perhaps a thermos of hot coffee, and then as one got home and had to put the horse away, that first drink — what should it be, such a noble thirst should not be wasted on just anything? A long draught of beer, an iced gin and tonic (oddly enough as often as not I ended up with straight orange juice) and then a wallow in a hot bath with plenty of pine essence in it, and finally the after dinner port with no fear of the extra couple of glasses, 'Earn your port and it won't hurt you.'

The best experience of all is that rare monemt when you have been sent ahead to watch one corner of a covert, and standing quite still you see Charles James stealing out looking back at the clamour of the hounds far behind. You hardly dare breathe and with luck your horse stays still until he's gone fifty yards — don't halloo yet, leave him another fifty — now he's clear and you stand in your stirrups and hold your hat high in the air and let out a View Halloo to wake the dead. You hold the 'Ho' till all your breath goes out; Tom's horn answers as he hurries the pack onto you with the 'gone away' call.

As the hounds get to the scent they break into a glorious clamour and surge out beside you.

'Which way, sir?' 'There he goes, just over the brow,' and you pick up your reins and put in your heels.

SHOOTING

The first time that I ever handled a shot gun was a few months after I came here in the winter of 1930. I was asked to shoot up at a farm called Bigods, and I borrowed a gun from old Mr Hasler and did not even open the case until I arrived. I did not know how to assemble it, and was fumbling ineffectively when one of the beaters quietly walked up and put it together for me. He was the roadman, and I saw him almost daily for the next forty years; he sometimes came and beat for me at Tilty. We never referred to the incident again, but there was a quiet bond between us.

Taffy Gwynn, the editor of the *Morning Post*, and Field Marshal Robertson from the First World War shared the shoot; among the guests was a magnificent character by name the Baron Marchienne de Cartier, the Belgian ambassador and doyen of the ambassadorial corps. He was dressed in a very dark old fashioned Norfolk suit, a wideawake hat and a large flowing cloak, and he was a brilliant shot. I drew the gun next to him, told him I was a beginner, so he let me have a bang or two and then took my birds as well as his own. At one stand, between Outlets and Dow Wood, standing on the road, he asked me if he had enough cartridges — he had twenty-nine. I assured him that they would be ample as it was a small wood, but the birds screamed out mostly over him, and suddenly he let out a stentorian roar of 'Stop ze shoot.' His man ran over to get a handful of cartridges out of my bag, and then the beaters came again but very little now came over.

I apologised, and asked how many he had down. He replied, 'Twenty eight — I had to shoot one twice.'

I did score one bird at that shoot, my first. I remember my astonishment when I saw it collapse in mid-air; I also shot a partridge with great pride, but it was walking up in a field of roots.

That was also my first experience of partridges, which were much commoner in Essex in the days before combines. After the corn had been cut it was stooked and left for some time before being pitched onto waggons, the stubble was left ten inches or more longer, and often not ploughed until November or even spring. So there was marvellous cover on the stubbles for the coveys of partridges, and a chance to walk within range by dodging from stook to stook. Insect life had not yet been poisoned by insecticides so that young partridges had plenty to eat for their first fortnight, and one reckoned about two birds to the acre as being a reasonable density of population. Later on, when I had shooting of my own, even 200 acres meant quite a number of partridges to be shot.

I had no lack of help and encouragement when I started shooting and the first to take me in hand was Cecil Welch. He was a good, careful shot, an ideal schoolmaster, and he had three or four hundred acres at the back of his house, including a good covert. We started on rabbits, of which there were swarms; on frosty mornings they would be hidden up in the tussocks of the rough meadows, and in the stubs of hedge alongside the ditches. He had a splendid little Jack Russell terrier called Grippy who was ideal for hunting them out, and old Paveling the keeper had a black labrador who worked in perfect harmony with the terrier. On their own they had developed the technique of the terrier working the ditch side of the stubs, and bolting the rabbit out where the labrador would be ready and waiting. We used to go down one on each side of the ditch with Grippy between us, and he had an uncanny knack of knowing when the rabbit had gone straight on down the ditch; he would come out and run outside as hard as he could for thirty or forty yards then dive in and bring the rabbit back towards us, and time and again it worked. Mr Welch was an absolute certain dead shot, while I usually missed and this puzzled the little dog. A shot from his master always meant something to retrieve; with me, he would hear my shot and come back looking puzzled, hunting for where the dead rabbit should be and not understanding. When I missed a couple of easy ones in succession, the next thing I heard was a squealing in the ditch, and he had decided to do the job himself! After a few months he fathered a litter of puppies, and I had one whom I called Whisky who was with me until the beginning of War.

I used to go out and practise on the lawn with a couple of dummy cartridges, swinging at small birds, swallows and the occasional pigeon, giving then the lead that I thought I should, following through as I pulled the trigger and slowly getting accustomed to the feel of the gun. Mr Hasler was very kind and let me keep the gun until I had one of my own, at the beginning of the War. This was a beautiful Holland & Holland, built just about the time that I was born, 1904, when guns were really made as works of art. It cost me exactly £45!

It never occurred to me in those days to keep a Game Book; I regret it now as I was invited to such marvellous shoots. Through Daphne I had got to know the estate at Quendon Hall well (we got engaged there just before a Hunt Ball) and I used to be asked to shoot there two or three times a year. It was splendid practice, beacuse if you missed one bird there would be several over you again in a matter of seconds. The bags used to be in the nature of 300, and after a bit I got reasonably efficient. The occasional right and left gave me confidence. I remember once shooting a high bird well ahead of me and thinking, 'They often fall near you but they can't hit you,' and at the last minute jumping aside as it landed on my open shooting stick and snapped half the seat off. I also remember standing in a line where I was high up and my next door neighbour was way down below me. Very high birds began to come over, and several times I missed one clean with both barrels only to have Tom 'wipe my eye' and bring it down behind me, and he must have been at least ten feet lower than I was.

Another time we were lining well away from a high belt of trees over which they were driving the pheasants; there was a real gale in our faces and suddenly a covey of partridges came over the plantation looking like a flock of starlings in the sky. Straight over me, so I gave them about three farm gates' lead and swung for all I was worth and fired. I had taken the leading bird, and the last one fell stone dead. Loud congratulations, and I didn't let on.

Lady Foot Mitchell was often one of the guns. She was fairly blind and pretty wild, and I used to hear the beaters as they neared us talking to each other, 'Where's her Ladyship standing?'

'Plumb opposite you, bor.'

'Oh, pray — you go on, I'll bide here a bit.'

She was always very hot on us not to shoot any red squirrels. Yet I saw her once to my amazement up with her gun, bang, and down one dropped. At the end of the drive it was duly picked up and laid out with the birds.

'Who shot that?'

When no-one replied, 'Well, you are all a lot of cowards, and I hope whoever it is is really ashamed of himself.'

My great trouble with Whisky was that he would work too fast ahead especially if the pheasant or rabbit ran on down a ditch: time and again I used to see the rabbit bolt a hundred yards ahead with Whisky hot on its heels, and any pheasants that were lurking in the ditch would have flown out as well long before I could get in range. I never could cure him of it, although I tried hard. Braintree Road carried very little traffic in those pre-war days, and I would put Whisky out at the top of the hill and drive to the corner before turning down to the farm, two miles or so, with this little white dot away in the distance following as fast as his legs could carry him. I thought that might tire him a bit but I found it only freshened him up! The only way was to have a companion who would take his gun wide of the ditch one or two hundred yards on, so that there was a chance of one or other of us getting a shot. I particularly remember one afternoon in the War when I was sent out by Daphne to 'go and get a pheasant' and carefully walked towards one of the little ditches which ran out into the field and then stopped suddenly right in the middle. I thought if I could get the pheasants into that and tie up Whisky and gently walk it out on my own, I might have a chance of several, but I had reckoned without him. Just as I was about to whistle him up and put him on the lead, he got the scent of a cock pheasant, was off like a flash, straight up to the ditch and he must have put out half a dozen birds well out of range and left me to return empty-handed.

Whisky ended a long and happy life under a motor car. Old Whybrow the gardener used to take letters and parcels to the post at four o'clock, and Whisky would go with him. On this occasion he took the corner too fast and swung off the pavement and onto the road, straight under a passing car. Without a shooting dog I was lost, but a formidable patient of mine, Lady Angela Erskine, had a pair of labradors from which she was just starting breeding. I put in for a puppy bitch, bought three, and picked the one I liked best, reselling the other two. There was an old retired keeper who lived up at Tilty and I gave the puppy to him to train when it was six months old. I went to see it once or twice and was puzzled at its lack of progress, but my old friend the roadman who had put my gun together at the first shoot and was a neighbour of the keeper, told me to take the dog away if I wanted it to be any good as he kept it in a kennel for eleven hours of the day and only had it out for one short walk. This accounted for her dazed behaviour, so I took her straight away and within a week she was a changed dog. I decided to train her myself and never regretted it. She was utterly willing and devoted and became that rare dog that would both hunt a hedge steadily when rough shoting and sit quietly at one's peg on a driving day. Her only technical fault was that she would 'run in' (that is to say, the moment she saw a bird falling she would run to collect it), and when I was shooting one day with McMullen at Canfield he complained that it taught other dogs bad manners. The next bird to fall was a strong cock that was only winged. It fell with a crash, picked itself up and was about to run off into the next parish when Dinah just caught him. I said to him,

'There, you see — your dog sent in due course to retrieve that bird wouldn't ever have had a chance.' I suppose part of my trouble was that too many of my birds were not killed cleanly but she made up for my shortcomings.

During the war I was given some more free shooting, this time at Tilty, I had some lovely days up there, because not only was it good partridge country, but there was also a wood with quite a number of wild pheasants, and rabbits galore. Next door to the wood were the remains of Tilty abbey, in a grass field with cattle grazing, and the little church which had been part of the abbey still standing. It is hilly out there, unlike much of flat Essex. In September after shooting partridges we would often take a picnic out and the children would join us.

Dinah had four litters of puppies, all of whom went to good homes. One litter stands out in my memory because Daphne had been putting bone meal on the rose bed just before I let them out one morning. They put their little noses in the air, and followed the delicious smell under the bushes where they proceeded to lap up this manna from heaven, and for weeks afterwards they always paid a first call there to see if anything more had arrived. I made a great mistake in not keeping one of the last lot she had when she was eight. I thought I could breed from her again, but alas she got growths on her nipples and had to be operated on and it was out of the question to make her pregnant again. So I had to look about for another dog again before she finally went, and a friend whose daughter had fallen ill in Paris and whom I had looked after, there, had a springer spaniel bitch and offered to breed from her from any dog of my choosing. I asked John Lukies for a service from his marvellous dog, and in due course Tara arrived. She was a splendid little dog, and I trained her myself but I never broke her of the habit of going in too fast just as Whisky had done. She hunted the ditches extremely well, and she retrieved anything, but she would not stay pegged at my stand to shoot and so disgraced me that I soon gave up trying. Once more I had to use the same technique of sending a gun on ahead, and by now I usually had one or two of the boys to come with me. My old friend Mr Lampl gave me the shooting over Brands Farm, and I had that for nearly twenty years and got to know every inch of it. That was best when the sugar beet was nearly ready to be harvested in late October and early November; walking slowly through with two or three dogs one put up what appeared deceptively easy shots, but they were very good practice for the boys to learn on. At first I had to wait while

122

one of them missed with both barrels, then I could finally take a great long shot and bring the bird down for the pot, but in time they got better. It was this walking round the rough shoot with Tara that I really enjoyed, though many people very kindly asked me for their set shoots.

Half a dozen year's after Dinah's death, I was shooting at Ravens when a golden labrador put her head in my hand as we were lunching, and I said,

'Whose dog is this? She reminds me of old Dinah.' Dinah had a distinctive snipey face with a dip from her forehead to her nose. I had not known this dog's owner, who lived some distance away, and he assured me that there could be no relation, but I persisted and asked where he had got her from and it turned out that I had originally sold her grandmother to a former friend. This friend's daughter still had one of her descendants and promised to breed a puppy for me, which she did in due course and so the second Dinah arrived, and proved every bit as good as the first. I thought I knew enough now to be able to train her myself, and everything went well: when I got her out she would hunt and retrieve extremely well but would not give the bird to my hand, laying it instead at my feet. Naturally if the bird was lightly pricked and still active it would jump up and run away, with Dinah in pursuit: occasionally it found the safety of a hedge and then we usually lost it. I tried various methods of curing her and they all failed, so I took her over to a trainer near Newmarket to see what he could do with her. After a couple of months he had made very little headway; she was willing and obedient and a good retriever but she would lay it down and he told me it was no good and I could come and take her away. I went over and talked to him and he said he would give her one more trial, and at the end of two or three weeks he rang to say that he had been successful. What he did was this. He had an alley between two hedges down which he used to make dogs run after retrieving to him standing at the far end, so for Dinah he put a small jump at this end just in front of him, so that she landed exactly where he stood. A dog always holds the bird while jumping, so he took it from her at once as soon as she touched down. Having done this for hours on end, he slowly lessened the height of the jump, until finally there was none, and it worked. For many years now she has always brought the game straight back to hand without

123

hesitation. I tried to breed from her, but it was a disaster, ending up with only one puppy which was drowned tragically in my swimming pool when I was suddenly called away in an emergency. The Dinahs had a bold temperament, and took reproaches quite philosophically, whereas my latest dog, Lilla is very different — sensitive to the last degree so that even a cross word will be enough to subdue her. The advantage is that she comes at once when called and will keep her eye on me for further orders even when she is looking for a bird at a distance. As I get older I value this instant obedience enormously, and it reminds me of all the extremely bad dogs belonging to other people that I have come across.

One famous one was a black labrador which belonged to a retired admiral. His wife had given it him as a birthday present, and it was quite uncontrollable, and if he could leave it behind when he went shooting, he would. One day he arrived rather late at 'Rab' Butler's shoot, explaining that his wife had stopped him as he drove out of the yard telling him that he had forgotten the dog. Reluctantly, he had brought him along, but of course had no lead. This was supplied, but looked to me rather flimsy, which it proved in due course. The dog behaved quite well in the morning; indeed, it was not allowed to do anything else: but in the afternoon the plan was to walk in a series of fields down into the central wide stretch of rough ground, which would then finally be brought forward over us at the end. The guns walked slowly in line towards the rough, taking a field at a time on either side and shooting nothing that went forward but only if they tried to break at the sides or back over us. We ended with quite a large number of partridges down in the rough, and very quietly assembled at the end for the final drive with the beaters coming down the far end. That is when it happened. Our friend the admiral was not holding on to his dog very tightly when a hare got up almost at his feet. The dog dashed away and the hare streaked straight down the rough with Remus yelping his head off in mad pursuit. Partridges rose in clouds streaming everywhere except over us and the admiral was so confused that he left early.

Another such dog was a springer spaniel which belonged to a tenant who came to live at Moor End and wanted the shooting which I had had previously. As I still had the neighbouring shoot of Tilty, he agreed that it would be a pity to break it up and that we would have shooting days together: this worked well except for his dog over which he had no control at all. He was a fairly stout middle-aged man, and could not move very fast: so he bought a strong lead and attached it to his braces button, and the dog towed him along. When a bird fell the dog would jump but the lead held until again a hare got up at his feet, and this time the button broke. The dog went one way and my friend went head over heels in the other direction. I discovered later that my eldest son had been offered a fiver by another gun to shoot the dog if the opportunity arose. This happened when it got loose and chased a hare past him. However, Nicolas thought discretion was the order of the day, in spite of the £5 offer and did not shoot.

The third in the trio was a very attractive old clumber spaniel, a breed which one does not associate with running in. He belonged to a very great friend of mine who used to come and hunt along the hedges out at High Easter. I soon learned that his stubborn disregard of his master's calls more than compensated for not being so fast: on the scent of a pheasant in a ditch he would go straight off at his own pace, but he always put the bird out hundreds of yards ahead of us. The only solution was to leave the pair of them behind while I walked right ahead, put a handkerchief in the ditch as a stop, and waited. This worked reasonably well but with a high hedge the pheasant was bound to break on the blank side and one could not always get a shot at it.

The cream of the shooting that I have had was from the early 1950s onward until I had to go easy; several farmers were very kind and let me have their land either free or for very small rents, and most of this I would use for rough shooting with my boys and one or two of their friends, not more than half a dozen, and walking the hedges with someone sent ahead at the end. When we had two good dogs we would work independently; and the odd railway cutting at one farm was a marvellous thick overgrown place for pheasants. The only trouble was the steep sides when you had to walk them half-way down. It was the best place, but after a bit you did long for one leg to be half the length of the other one. On our best days there we would get thirty or more birds and almost as many rabbits as we wanted.

Before that I had the Tilty land, with Goodfellows, Moor

125

End and Coldharbour added to it which came to nearly a thousand acres, and here the partridges were particularly good. There was a drive over a huge field called Buckle Shoe with a stream running at the far end, and the beaters went into the field beyond that and slowly brought it over the stream and us behind the hedge at the top. They were splendid partridges, and I used to watch in envy and astonishment at the way that Frank Cock used to take his brace always in front, firing the first shot long before I thought the birds could possibly be in range.

Once my brother-in-law and I were walking through some high roots, and two coveys of partridges got up. Between us we had seven birds down; it was a hot, dry day, Dinah was working well, and we spent at least half an hour looking for them and retrieved one. Beaters were always a problem, particularly on Boxing Day. We did not want to hunt as it was really only a social outing so I decided to cover the huge area of ground with the beaters on horses. Philippa and I and two children and a couple of friends, one of whom was accompanied by an energetic and indefatigable standard poodle, covered the large fields easily, and put up masses of partridges. Surprisingly most of them flew over the guns, but unfortunately they got up a long way away and were going too high and too fast. They looked line starlings and although there were some good shots in the line few came down.

Twice I remember being put in a 'double bank'. Once was at Quendon where the drive narrowed down so that only four guns could shoot abreast, and our host put the other four a couple of gunshots behind them with strict instructions to the front rank only to take birds ahead. The other time was in Kent where two woods converged at the head of a valley and rides were cut two thirds of the way up. The guns lined these rides and between them, and then I was led all by myself right up to the apex where the woods joined. My host said to me:

'You'll get a lot of shooting here, all the birds that go over those guns will come on over you.' I felt very lonely up there for a long time as the beaters came towards the guns lower down, and then the birds started coming ahead. Several came down, but more flew over me, and I had a very busy quarter of an hour.

In recent years I have only been out for half days when it is fine and warm, but from my consulting room window upstairs I have a grandstand view of the courtship and subsequent behaviour of the pheasants. In early spring there will be one or two old cocks with his attendant seven or eight hens, and young cocks skirmishing on the fringe and being chased away with loud crows by the cock in possession. I have seen one fly away squawking, but only to go round the house in a circle and land right in the middle of the hens where he will make himself agreeable while the cock struts back congratulating himself, only to find the interloper and chase him off the other way again. Eventually they settle down with two or three hens apiece, and when it comes to nesting time the habits change. Twice a day, morning and evening, the hens will be told to take a break, and will fly out on to the young field of wheat stretching to the horizon for half an hour to stretch their legs and peck around. Suddenly the cocks will look up and say, 'Come on girls, back to the job, time's up,' and chase them back into their wood or hedge, after which they will retrace their steps leisurely two and two together like amiable old gentlemen out for a stroll. Then each will come back to perch on his point of vantage where he can stand and warn the hens of any approaching danger and fend off intruders. From time to time he gives a crow with a curious muffled ruffling of his feathers. When hatching is approaching the cocks go quiet and you see or hear little more of them until the corn is cut and the young broods are out on the stubbles. I had been brought up to the idea that the cock was a very bad father and took little interest in the hens and chicks once the hens began nesting, but I realise how wrong I was.

Towards evening rabbits poke their noses out of the edge of the wood and the bolder ones come out to feed in the meadow in the failing light. Sometimes these pay the penalty of their boldness to my .22 Walther with a telescopic sight from the rifle of a German sniper in the First World War. Once I had ten rabbits with successive shots between fifty or sixty yards away, but since then word has got round and they don't come nearer than a hundred yards which is an uncertain range.

One of the reasons why my father gave up shooting was that as he got older he disliked the idea of taking life. I have found that this is shared by several older men, and I now think that way myself; but I still like to hear from younger friends how the season's shooting is going.

EPILOGUE

Once when I was looking for an extra partner, I was asked what sort of qualities I was after; and I said: 'I think I want a chap who is always prepared to cope with an impossible situation. Someone who might have a raging temperature or a frightful hangover, woken up in the middle of the night with an indistinct message down the telephone to visit someone he had never heard of and with the vaguest address. Snow and fog and a puncture, and when he did find the house and the patient, he was prepared to cope with an illness he couldn't diagnose with what he happened to have in his bag; not ask the registrar to help him, or go back like the plumber for his tools.'

A prescription for health

Take an apple a day
Eat it each morning on the back of a horse
Watching the sun rise.